A COVERT MILITARY THRILLER

TOBIN'S WAR

SWAMP WAR

CALIBER
BOOKS

Also from ALAN CAILLOU

CABOT CAIN Series
    Assault on Kolchak
    Assault on Loveless
    Assault on Ming
    Assault on Agathon
    Assault on Fellawi
    Assault on Almata

TOBIN'S WAR Series
    Dead Sea Submarine
    Terror in Rio
    Congo War Cry
    Afghan Assault
    Swamp War
    Death Charge
    The Garonsky Missile

MIKE BENASQUE Series
    The Plotters
    Marseilles
    Who'll Buy My Evil
    Diamonds Wild

IAN QUAYLE Series
    A League of Hawks
    The Sword of God

DEKKER'S DEMONS Series
    Suicide Run
    Blood Run

The Charge of the Light Brigade
A Journey to Orassia

Rogue's Gambit
Cairo Cabal
Bichu the Jaguar
The Walls of Jolo
The Hot Sun of Africa
The Cheetahs
Joshua's People
Mindanao Pearl
Khartoum
South from Khartoum
Rampage
The World is 6 Feet Square
The Prophetess
House on Curzon Street

TOBIN'S WAR: SWAMP WAR
Book Five

For further information visit the Caliber Comics website:
www.calibercomics.com

Cover Art by Alexandr Timofeev

MEET THE PRIVATE ARMY

Once, when the natives got restless, as they used to say in the old days, there was always a stock answer: *send in the troops!*

They called it gunboat diplomacy and, in its time, it worked. The moral question never seemed to come up. The boats sailed up the river, the soldiers landed, fixed their bayonets, and charged...

A few villages were blown up, and a lot of people were hanged, to teach them a lesson; and it never seemed to matter very much if they were the *right* people. Often as not, they weren't.

And the world was safe a little longer for Democracy. The widows mourned their husbands, children mourned their fathers, but it didn't matter anymore; the avenging angels were back in their smug homes again. What could they care about rivers running with other people's blood?

From India to Puerto Rico, from China to Dominica, from Africa to Viet Nam; the pattern was the same.

Not anymore.

Today, the delicate fabric of international diplomacy is too fragile, and the spark of internal dissent carries with it the flame of worldwide war, and *that*, we all know, means annihilation for all of us. Besides, the natives don't fight with spears anymore; they use, instead, the tanks and the guns that we gave them...

But the dissent is still there. Sometimes it is justified. Often, it is not. All over the world, the extreme groups, on either flank, can and do still bring frightening menace into all our lives—the fear of a spreading conflagration which may never end until we are, all of us, and our children, dead.

And yet, if the evil is identified and caught in time...

A handful of skilled and dedicated men could have stopped Attila the Hun *before* he got strong enough to bring half of Europe to its knees. They could have stopped Genghis Khan before he brought havoc to all of Asia. They could have stopped Napoleon, or Hitler, or Stalin, if they'd caught them in time. The destruction of these violent men would have been halted before it got under way; and then, who knows what course the world would have taken? We can only know that it would have been a much safer place for us to live in.

The problem? How do you recognize the danger for what it is, and what do you do about it?

The answer? *You call in the Private Army of Colonel Tobin.*

Colonel Tobin is real. That's not his name, but he exists.

He has gathered about him a small and tightly-knit band of experts from all over the world—Americans, Englishmen, Chinese, Germans, Russians, Cubans, Czechs, Frenchmen, Israelis, Arabs, it doesn't matter where they come from as long as they're the best in the world. They are specialists, as the Colonel is, in cutting out the cancer of evil before it becomes virulent and chaos takes over completely.

They are hard-headed professional soldiers, all of them. As Colonel Tobin says: "That happy time has not yet come when we can do without our Armies. When it does, I'll disband mine, and no man will be better pleased. Until then—I get in there first, and I hit the hardest. I work quickly, efficiently, and in secret...And I use the rapier instead of the broadsword..."

Have the guerrillas of El Fatah found a sure-fire way to destroy Israel, almost overnight? Then call in Colonel Tobin!

Are the white mercenaries making a battlefield of the Congo? Then call in Colonel Tobin.

Is Brazil on the brink of civil war? Then send for the Colonel...

He is shrewd, knowledgeable, and the best tactician in history. He is a welcome guest at all foreign ministries but they'd rather he use the back door, please, and keep his voice down.

Tobin is in his late fifties, a slight, wiry man with the restless air of a prowling animal about him, and a brain to match the computers in his oak-paneled study. His eyes are pale and blue, and they size you up and down, and God help you if he decides that you are the enemy.

He is as tough as a barrel full of shrapnel, sharp and incisive, and a man to reckon with. He is a hard-drinking martinet, with a bottle of his favorite Irish whisky always close by. It's his trademark, and if you're in trouble in the middle of nowhere, with the enemy pressing you hard, and you find an empty Irish bottle lying around—then you can relax. The Colonel is close by and your deadliest worries are over. "You can drink what you damn well like," he says to his men, "and as much as you damn well like. Only God help the man I ever find drunk. Ever..."

He has a son, Major Paul Tobin, not much more than a kid, tousled-haired and freckled and handsome; and the best damn fighting-man since Alexander.

He has an aide, whom he calls, sardonically, "my man Charles." Her name is indeed Charles, Pamela Charles, and she's thirty-three years old, five-foot ten, a woman—*all* woman—of astonishing beauty, the longest legs ever, with a taste for see-through dresses. She is his memory-bank, his personal servant, his confidante, his masseuse, a stimulus to his imaginings—and she's anything else the Colonel wants her to be.

There's Betty de Haas, the best cartographer who ever came out of the legendary Royal College of Holland, a tight-bodied little brunette of twenty-seven who lives above the Colonel's office with all her charts and maps and satellite photos, in a made-over attic with green and white rafters and a well-used bed.

He has Rick Meyers, historian, a quiet and erudite man with a dark, enquiring mind and a great love of the intelligence upon which efficient warfare is founded.

And Major Bramble, a great bear of a man who can't keep his eyes off Betty's plump little breasts, and a ferocious battler who fears neither man nor devil.

There's craggy old Cass Fragonard, a veteran of the Algerian wars, who runs on two tin legs—he lost his own in the Sahara Desert—better than a teenager. He's a gruff old Frenchman who lives on the best cognac his beloved France can provide.

There's Ahmed Idriss, once archer-instructor to the sons of the late King Said Idriss el Senussi of Libya, a desert Bedouin who can have five shafts in the air from his handmade bow before the first strikes home. He is astonishingly accurate, always on target.

There's Edgars Jefferson, the black man from Chicago, physically Tobin's strongest man, and a terror if he doesn't like you, yet the best friend a man could have if he does.

There's Mendoza the Mexican, Manuel the Brazilian, the Icelander from Reykjavik who calls himself Alaric, cool, silent and deadly. There's Sergeant Roberts, who once climbed Annapurna in spite of his bloody hernia, and Efrem Collas the Israeli, who moves in the dark like a leopard, and Gopa the Ghurka and Subahat Singh the Sikh, and Hamash the Turk who lost a foot to a submarine's propeller in the Dead Sea...

And all over the world, in every potential trouble-spot, there's a man—or woman—secretly gathering the facts that Rick Meyers will feed into those computers to chart the course of the world's worries.

They are banded together, these people and others, bound by a strong and devoted loyalty to the Colonel; because he's the first General in history to insist that the lives of his men are sacred...They know that they'll never be wasted.

They live, work; fight, drink and love like devils, these people. Wherever they may be in a hostile world, they know the Colonel is close by, watching out for them, setting them tasks that are not impossible because—they know—his skill and his tenacity are with them. Each man, on his own; is an expert— deadly expert. And together they make up the smallest, the tightest, the most efficient fighting force the world has ever known.

They are the PRIVATE ARMY OF COLONEL TOBIN.

CHAPTER 1

Okaloacoochee Slough.

Coordinates: 81.01E
                    26.32N

There was the evil, unholy smell of death in the Swamp.

It seemed to hang in the gray mist that rose up out of the wet ground, and to drape itself from the long cattails of Spanish moss that festooned the trees. Even the trees themselves reeked of it; they were gaunt and stark, and seemed to belong to another age, to another planet. Although crowded together, each individual tree was nevertheless an entity, a symbol, a menace, its long roots reaching out as though to search and destroy...

The croaking of the frogs was constant and loud, as though they too were aware of the imminence of evil, as though it frightened them.

There was no sun here. Somewhere out there, no doubt, the sun brightened a cleaner sky, but here, under the damp canopy of dark green and gray foliage, which it could not penetrate, there was only the fog and the damp and the cold. The smell was of rotting wood, of humus, and of decaying sludge. It was a fearful, oppressive place, where nothing that was clean could ever live.

The four captives, three young men and a girl, were

struggling through the knee-deep water, their wrists tightly bound behind their backs, the long rope that joined them cutting into their necks, drawing blood with its chafing. They had been beaten, all of them, even the girl, because beating, and even death, was part of the discipline that had been imposed and would never be relaxed not while Simon Kirby was still alive.

The girl was weeping now. Just a kid with long, untidy hair that was seldom washed or combed, and a sort of lost, bewildered expression on her child's face, she was scared beyond belief, not understanding in the least that what she had done to others could happen to her. She said, whimpering, "I didn't do anything—haven't done anything wrong..."

Someone close by, one of the guards, said brutally, "You got yourself knocked up. You think a pregnant broad can fight? You know it's against the rules."

The young man behind her, his dark, angry eyes now glazed over, his fear and incomprehension evident, muttered, "My God, this is America—this is the twentieth century—it can't happen, it can't..."

A whip cracked, and the stinging tail of it flicked out and opened a wound between his shoulder blades; the whip, too, was part of the discipline.

He turned and yelled now, a fury of panic, his voice hoarse and broken, "What's the matter with you, you mother—"

One of the guards, the one with the whip, stepped forward and yanked on the neck-rope, pulling it tight and throwing the young man to the ground. He screamed, and the guard stepped on the back of his head; forcing his face into the slime and holding it there, watching his frantic threshing. Then he yanked him to his feet, kicked him in the groin, and said, "Nothing's the matter with me. How do *you* feel?" The girl had fallen too. The guard pulled her up and pushed her on, and the little column struggled forward.

Beside them, the two dugouts were laden with armed

men. They were cutting silent ripples through the water, a man in the stern of each with a long pole, punting them along. The moss hung down to the water, and from time to time the dugouts just disappeared into the lush greenery, reappearing again in menacing silence—always in silence—a little further on. The rich smell of the swamp was sulphuric, the smell of rotting eggs.

The guard gestured with his rifle, "There, over there, get with it." He hated the swamp, hated the stench and the damp and the loneliness of it, but he had taken the oath that they had all taken, and this was his home now, his home for as long as this hopeless task would last. He took a kind of masochistic pleasure in suffering it for the Cause, and he thrust his hatred behind him.

He too was young, perhaps twenty-seven or twenty-eight years old, and he limped badly; a police bullet, three years ago, had crippled him, and he had never forgiven them for it. True, at the time he had been killing another policeman, but that he regarded as his right. After all, that was at least part of what the Organization was about; and now, the CAAA was the whole of his life. He reveled in its hatreds, in its violence, and in its dreadful, distorted sense of power. He was dressed in a sort of uniform of cotton drab, and he prodded with his rifle again and said, "There, on the bank, you bastard."

The Major was there, in one of the boats, Major Simon Kirby. He was standing up in the prow, tall, rugged, battle-scarred, a black patch over his left eye. Once, perhaps, he had been handsome, but now the face was too cruel, too hard, for good looks. There were deep lines at the sides of his mouth, and a bitter, sardonic glint in the one eye. He turned to look at the column of prisoners, then looked at the guards behind them, checking the way they moved, the way they carried their weapons as they splashed through the water in careless open order. He said angrily, "Close up there—get into line. Where the hell do you think you are?"

They carried their Kalashnikov submachine guns loosely,

and there were grenades from the same factory hanging from their belts. Long ago, in Algeria, Japan, Libya, and Chile, it had been decided by the men who ruled Simon Kirby's destiny that the Kalashnikov was the most reliable weapon, the most easily obtainable, the most easily replaceable. There was another reason too; since it was Russian design, it put the Soviets in a position, *vis-à-vis* the American enemy, that could only be regarded as blameworthy, and that was an added bonus. The guards were carrying machetes, too, and they slashed their way into the shrubbery. One of them carried a load of landmines, slung on his shoulders in an aluminum carrier.

The little column struggled up onto firm land, and the two canoes were motionless. The guards, six of them, gathered around and pushed the prisoners against one of the giant cypress trees that had given this part of the swamp its name. The young man shouted, "You're not going to get away with it, you know that, don't you?" Someone hit him in the face, very hard, with a fist, and broke his nose. The Major stepped lightly ashore, holding himself very straight as he moved, and said wryly, "We *have* gotten away with it, friend."

They were tying the prisoners tightly with a length of electrical wire around their throats—a single wire around four necks and the trunk of the cypress—so tightly that they could hardly breathe, the four of them close together and struggling uselessly. The girl was sobbing now.

The Major pulled a paper from his pocket and waved it at them. "You don't want me to read this, do you, you know what it's all about."

He read it anyway, in patches, grunting, commenting on it: "Jerry Devlin, Hans Schneidre, Carlos Amana, Margaretta Santana. By the authority vested in me by the CAAA, you all know what that is, or have you forgotten?" He stepped forward and said savagely to one of them, "You forgot, you sonofabitch, didn't you?" He hit him hard across the mouth with the flat of his hand, three times in rapid succession, and the young man spluttered blood and teeth at him, soiling the cotton drab. He said, "Okay, by the authority vested in me et cetera, et cetera, all four of you are sentenced to death by a duly appointed jury of the Committee, sentences to be carried out et cetera, et cetera. And if it's any consolation to you, I'm glad to see it happen. You're a bunch of weak-kneed, yellow-bellied punks; we don't have any room for you anymore. All you're good for is a lesson to anyone else who thinks the discipline's too tough. Okay, Lieutenant, you know what to do, so do it."

He stepped back and lit a cigarette, and the Lieutenant came forward with a twig he had cut with his bush knife. He sighed. He was a good-looking young man in his late twenties, a face too old for his years, with dark, beetling brows drawn in a perpetual frown and a long, drooping moustache. He came from Chile, and he too hated the swamp; but for him too, this was his life now; he too had sworn allegiance, and besides, there was the money going back home to his wife. Would he ever see her again?

He patted the young girl's breast, lifting it up in his cupped hand as though weighing it, and said; "Seems a pity, the girl I mean." His English was faintly accented. He looked at the Major, and Kirby said shortly, "You want to take her place, Lieutenant, that's all right with me. I'll finish you both off myself."

The Lieutenant shrugged. He was not in the least scared of Simon Kirby, though everyone else in the outfit seemed to be. He jiggled the sobbing girl's breast and said drily; "That's a great boob, Okay."

He walked to the back of the tree, and slipping his twig under the wire, began twisting it round and round, drawing the wire tighter and tighter. Their legs were thrashing wildly, and the Major said curtly; "Too fast, ease off." He slackened the tension for a moment and then took it up again. When it was good and tight, he wedged it in position, walked around to the front again, and watched them, squatting down on his heels and looking up at their purple, bloating faces. He found it extraordinary, even comic, that the young girl's tongue was reaching out of her gaping mouth. A cap fell from one of her teeth, and her eyes were rolling back; there was blood at her throat, and she was still struggling. One of them, he saw, was already dead, and he saw the two others die. Only the girl was still alive. He laughed and looked up at the Major and said; "You see? She doesn't want to die either, look at her." He found it astonishing that anyone dead could hang on to the last vestiges of life so desperately. He said, "We don't have to bury them, do we?"

Simon Kirby shook his head slowly, "Plenty of birds and insects around; all living creatures need fresh meat."

She had ceased her struggling. Her once pretty face was hideous now, a blotched blue and purple, with a red and swollen tongue, slimy and obscene. The Lieutenant got to his feet, felt for her heart, and said, "A dead boob now. It's a shame, isn't it?"

Kirby said, "The land mines. There, there, there, over there. Maybe they'd better be strung together, one goes off they all go off. Stick one of them between her legs, under her pants, a bonus for somebody."

He waited while the men set the land mines, very gingerly. Carolyne Southby had made them, and she was known to be fond of the hair trigger. They were copies of the old German Shu mines, but in plastic boxes instead of the well-made wooden cases the Germans had used, and they were packed with two pounds of TNT instead of the original half pound. He watched while they wired them together and slipped the last one down the dead girl's trousers, gently easing it around to the back where if could not be seen. He said, "Okay, safety catches off, take it easy now, they're delicate. One hand on the case, the other takes out the pin. You know the drill."

There was enough of the explosive in the eight mines to

blow them all to kingdom come. He stood there, immobile, and watched them at careful work. He collected the eight pins as a check and tossed them into the black water. "All right, we stay on the alert. Get back to Position Four."

He called the Lieutenant over and gave him the paper, saying, "Pin this up on the board." He had scrawled on it with the ballpoint: *Sentences carried out, signed, Simon Kirby, Major.* "And find Carolyne. Tell her to send a note to the pigs to come and get the bodies. I want one man up in a tree..." He looked around. "Up there, the mangrove. One man to see what happens. Maybe Strickland pays us another visit, who knows? Maybe he'll set of those mines—we might just get lucky. I want to know about it. Better be one of the Japanese."

The Lieutenant said, "Check."

"He can pick off a couple of them while he's at it."

"Check."

The Major looked over the waiting men. He jerked a thumb at the bodies and said, "Make good and sure everyone knows about this. Make sure they know what happens when the rules get broken. This is a military outfit, not just a bunch of Boy Scouts. I don't want anyone to forget that. Let's go."

He climbed aboard his waiting dugout, watched the men taking up their positions for the journey back, and nodded.

The dugouts began their silent journey back to the hideout and the frogs began croaking again.

CHAPTER 2

London.

Coordinates: 00.00E
              51.50N

Colonel Matthew Tobin was in a state of shock.

There was no other word for it. He could feel the apoplexy suffusing his face and was conscious that he was, perhaps, losing his customary aplomb—not completely, of course, but sufficiently to make him stammer if he were to open his mouth.

So he held his peace for a moment or two, and when his visitor began to speak again, he raised an authoritative hand for silence. All sound stopped.

The Colonel rose from the deep leather armchair and pushed a button on the console, "Charles?" he said quietly.

"Bring us some more coffee; would you please? And switch the Mark Four over to my study right away."

He looked at the beautiful brass ship's clock on the wall—ten-fifteen in the morning. A pale blue glow appeared on its face, indicating that the voice pattern machine, the new Mark Four still on the top secret list, had been switched on.

He turned back to his visitor, a bronzed, good-looking man in his late fifties, with neat silver-gray hair and a faintly amused half-smile on his lips. *A tough sonofabitch*, the Colonel was thinking, *don't be fooled by that too damn casual nonchalance.* He was wearing a double-knit suit that could have come from any of the best New York tailors, conservatively gray but a touch too mod for his age. He sat, perfectly at ease, on the arm of the leather sofa, sipping the very large Irish whiskey the Colonel had poured for him.

"It's a very good drink," the visitor said musingly, "perhaps I should switch to it." Was he being too nonchalant? Was he too deliberately trying for a calm that he did not feel? He said, "Yes, perhaps I'll do that," and the Colonel said abruptly, "Am I really supposed to believe that your name is Arthur J. Wagnall? Don't you think it might be better to tell me exactly who you are?"

The visitor shrugged. "Arthur J. Wagnall—it's the name they gave me, the name I always use on these missions. Would Admiral Henderson sound better?"

"Henderson, Henderson...Yes, possibly. But I'm still going to need to know one hell of a lot more about you before I commit myself to such a...such an atrocious undertaking."

"Then you are already committed in principle? If my credentials satisfy you?"

The Colonel said sharply, "No." He reached for the Irish in its crystal decanter, poured himself another drink, sighed, and said, "I am being invited to land an alien army on American soil, with, so you say, the express approval of 'the authorities,' whomever you might mean by that. I should add that I have never even heard of your Committee, and I am a well-informed man on these matters, Mr. Wagnall."

Wagnall was smiling still, very sure of himself. He looked around the elegant room with its beautiful woodwork, parchment lamp shades, priceless paintings. One long wall was filled with the huge console, most of it covered with exquisite walnut paneling, a few doors open to show the lights gleaming and the tape reel turning. It was the first time he'd seen a computer that looked like built-in furniture. The armchairs, the sofa, the divan, were of leather, suitably worn; there was a feeling of a luxurious St. James Street club.

"No, I don't suppose you ever have," Wagnall replied. "And for the same reason that very few people have heard of your Private Army...the trouble I had tracking you down! By their very nature, both our organizations have to operate with a considerable degree of secrecy. I'm sure you'll agree. And both are vital to the security not only of our own countries but of the world in general."

"But on American soil! Somehow, it doesn't seem...correct. Indeed, I find it preposterous."

"That, surely, is an inhibition that did not seem to cause you too much concern when you took your men to Israel. Or Afghanistan. Or the Congo. Or to any of a dozen other places."

There was a little silence before the Colonel spoke again. "And I also have an intense dislike of organizations that know too much about my own activities. The source of your information?"

"My Committee."

"Then kindly have your Committee mind its own damn business."

Mr. Wagnall said mildly, "We like to be kept well informed about what's happening in the dangerous world of the revolutionary fanatic. As I said, it's vital to all of us. When we heard from the Congo that the major war that was about to start there had inexplicably—how shall I put it?—had inexplicably fizzled out, we made certain inquiries. It seems our government thinks very highly of your capabilities. We made additional inquiries of your own government..."

The Colonel interrupted him, "And they told you nothing, I hope?"

"*Almost* nothing, I was switched from one office to

another, up and down Westminster's social scale, until at last I could make some sort of sense out of the information I was gradually being fed. Not much, you understand. Just a little here, a little there." He took a deep breath and said, "If you force me to use a name, will the Third Secretary at Number Ten suffice? George Merriman? And if you would like to call our Ambassador, he has already been told—in the vaguest possible terms—of my mission."

"That," the Colonel said, "is exactly what I will do. I'll leave the matter of your Committee for the moment; I'm quite sure I can find out all want to know about it from my own sources. But this...CAAA. I want to know more about that. From you. I want to know a great deal more."

There was a light knock on the door, and Charles came in with the coffee—a silver tray with two small eggshell cups of Stafford china and a silver coffeepot. The Colonel said airily, "I don't believe you've met Charles, have you?"

Wagnall got to his feet, feeling a little bewildered. Realizing that his mouth was foolishly open, he closed it, gulped, and forced a smile.

"This is Pamela Charles," the Colonel said, "my aide, my personal servant, my secretary, my confidante. She is completely *au courant* with all the affairs of this office, so please don't let your own inhibitions trouble you. " He looked at the secretary and said, "Charles, this is Mr. Arthur J. Wagnall, and he wants us to invade America. We just might do it—it's been a long time since I was there."

Wagnall stared. He thought that he had never in all his life seen so lovely a woman.

She was tall and svelte and blonde—and unbelievably sensual, with the longest legs he had ever seen. Her hair was piled high on the top of her head, and her neck was long and slim. Her eyes held his in a manner he found completely disconcerting, as though she were probing, sounding him out,

15

finding out for herself just what kind of man he really was. She wore long, white linen trousers, flared, with white sandals and a white silk halter, and her skin was the color and texture of alabaster. He had an extraordinary urge to reach out and touch her, and wondered if she had this effect on everybody. She put down the tray and smiled at him.

He took her hand and held it as she said, "A great pleasure, Mr. Wagnall." Then, turning to the Colonel, "Rena had some papers for you."

He nodded. Charles threw the switch on the desk that unlocked the door and lit the green lamp in the hall. A pretty, young girl came in, almost secretively, placed a file on the desk, and went quickly out again. While Pamela Charles poured the coffee, the Colonel picked up the file.

He speed-read the first two pages, noting the salient points and discarding the rest:

"Voice Print Report, X279, 82 ft. tape 5.5.73, Washington authority, radio, confirmation awaited, subject is Admiral Meredith Connolly Henderson, 6th Fleet, retired, now Personal Adviser to the President on Internal Security, head of the Committee of Alien Affairs, PS rating Double-A. Arrived U.K. from Washington 4.5.73, carrying a personal letter from the President to Colonel Tobin, a copy of which will follow. Age: 59, height 6'1", weight thirteen stone two, hair gray-white, complexion fair (usually bronzed), eyes hazel, nose straight, mouth large, lower lip protruding, chin bisected, left earlobe larger than right, fluent in French, German, Russian, adequate in Korean and has a working knowledge of Chinese script...possible contact with PA through Afghan Ambassador at U.N, personal friend of long standing of Brazilian President...Married, wife Leona May Dresden, who is a naturalized U.S. citizen of Czech origin, three sons, Henry, Martin and Paul, two latter killed in

Vietnam, first, youngest, Annapolis...Travels under the name Arthur J. Wagnall or Frederick Paulac. Subject's intellectual virtuosity is considered very high, he is known as a ladies' man, controlled, a moderate drinker, does not gamble, and is considered a very likely candidate for President or Vice in next election. General status and character very high. His secret phone number is 386-2179..."

He tossed down the file and saw that Wagnall, or Paulac, or the Admiral, could not take his eyes off Pamela Charles' breasts. They were chatting together like old friends, a knack that she had, and there was the little laugh that sounded not in the least artificial.

He pushed the console button that led to one of the hidden offices in the attic and said, "Mark Four off, please." The pale glow on the clock disappeared almost unnoticeably, and the Colonel said bluntly, "Well, my mind is by no means made up, Mr. Wagnall. But you were telling me about the CAAA."

He tore himself away. "Ah yes." He looked quickly at Charles, and the Colonel said again, smoothly, "My confidante. Perfectly all right to talk your head off."

"Yes, of course. Well..." He cleared his throat and continued, "The CAAA, the Committee for Anti-American Activities. We've known about it for a long time, of course, but until recently it's been an overseas problem, and hence not really my affair, though I've kept a watching brief on them because their leader was always an American citizen. Its aim seems to be the disruption of what might be called the better effects which our presence hopefully has on the rest of the world. But now, they're operating on American soil, and...It started with what is commonly called the People's Red Army in Japan, an extremely violent organization of fanatics. You may have heard of them?"

"I have."

"And when the Arab guerrillas first made contact with

them, the only immediate and apparent result was the massacre at Lod Airport by the three Japanese terrorists. You remember?"

"I do, indeed."

"But there were much more important ramifications of that initial approach. Somehow, the Tupamarus from Chile got into the act and found that they were pursuing the same general approach as the so called Red army..." He broke off and said mildly, "We never did discover why they chose that particular name. They are definitely not Communist."

The Colonel said, "They chose that name because in the early stages it was China that was supplying them with their arms. Now, they are equipped almost exclusively with the Russian Kalashnikov weapons—rifles, submachine guns, grenades, land mines... The choice of name was a sop to their friends, no more. No, they are not Communist, nor Fascist. They are terrorists, pure and simple."

"So...Then, somehow or other, a few of the more violent dissident groups in America, who had been working rather loosely with some Algerian expatriates, also got into the act. Among them was a man named Simon Kirby. American, forty years old, a vet from Korea and Vietnam, a thoroughly bad hat, convicted in a very unpleasant case of fragging. He escaped from jail and has been living in Algeria ever since. It seems that he too was making contact with the Japanese extremists for purposes of his own, joined their so-called Red Army when he found that they were more opposed to American influence than anything else, and finally..."

Pamela Charles was quietly refilling his glass, pouring his third Irish of the morning. As he looked at the soft curve of her breasts under the halter, the nipples erect and hard and showing clearly, he almost shuddered.

He said, "Thank you, my dear."

He looked back at the Colonel hurriedly, knowing that his looks were betraying him, and went on. "Finally, Simon Kirby put his very considerable organizational talents to work. You have to realize that he has an undying hatred of everything American, his own country. Something to do with what happened in Vietnam—we don't quite know what it was.

"He suggested to both the Japanese and the Tupos that they move onto American soil—the old maxim, it's always better to attack your enemy on his home ground. Previously, they'd been blowing up military aircraft, dropping bombs in airport fuel tanks, all that sort of thing. It seems that both groups listened to what Kirby had to offer and were highly impressed with his ability as a revolutionary leader. They talked it over among themselves—we have the transcript of the meeting they held in Rome—and finally decided to agree with his suggestions. He took a number of them, we don't know how many, to a hideout somewhere in the Everglades, in the swamps, and they started out on a course of simple assassination, not even always victims of any importance, but...Well, we suspect that he's was probing, showing his hand and trying to find out the skill and the determination of...the Establishment. And the Establishment, so far, hasn't done too well."

Wagnall paused to sip his drink, enjoying the smoky warmth of it in his throat, before continuing, somewhat ruefully. "There's a man named Strickland, Captain Strickland, Florida State Special Forces, an ex-Army Captain and as tough as they come, who now heads a semisecret detachment of State Police reinforced with federal and military muscle. Strickland was assigned the job of getting Simon Kirby and his men out of the swamps and bringing them to trial. Eight of his men were killed at the first attempt, six more the second time...He called in the National Guard, the proper thing to do under the authority that's been vested in him..." He scowled. "Three men killed, eleven wounded, and the rest of them damn near lost in that damned swamp. Kirby knows it like the back of his hand; he was born there and...Have you ever seen the Everglades, Colonel Tobin?"

19

The Colonel shook his head, and Wagnall grimaced and said, "A great tourist attraction. Spanish moss all over, hidden creeks that lead nowhere, great roots reaching out into black water. A few alligators to give the visitor a sense of vicarious danger...Now, the danger is a very real one. Kirby's in there with several hundred, perhaps several thousand men...Some women, too. And from time to time, he reaches out, reaches out a long way...He sends commando groups to Washington, to Boston, to Los Angeles, to Los Alamitos."

He sighed. "If he picked his targets less carefully, we'd have an immense weapon against him."

Colonel Tobin said swiftly, "Ah, yes, public opinion. Is that what you mean?"

"Exactly. If he had our ten top men assassinated, our best men, then there'd be an outcry that would enable us to use a little more muscle. But he won't do that. He strikes out, kills some poor inoffensive schmuck no one's ever heard of...Only that innocent schmuck happens to be a key man somewhere or other, a man whose importance far outweighs his public image. Two of Russia's top scientists, on a very, very secret and delicate mission to Miami, were blown to pieces last week. No one, at this early stage, had ever heard of them; the general public wasn't even aware that we were trying to collaborate with the Soviets in this particular field. But they were at work on a secret scientific accord with the United States that would have been a tremendous step forward. The incident made our security arrangements look inadequate, and the whole setup has been jeopardized. And Kirby gloats. It's another smack in the eye for the Administration, for the American image."

The Colonel grunted. Pamela Charles had settled herself in a corner and was quietly studying the file the young Rena had brought in, throwing an occasional glance at the two of them, listening unobtrusively.

The Colonel said at last, "Your information about

them...It's sketchy, but it seems to point to a source of Intelligence."

Wagnall nodded. "Yes, indeed. We put a man into the CAAA four months ago. It took him three months to work his way up to a position of trust. That's when they found him out. They killed him." Brooding, he said, "A good man, one of the best."

"But not good enough. Not an American characteristic, is it? Good Intelligence work requires a certain deviousness, a cunning, that is alien to your national character."

He said to Pamela Charles, "Get Betty in here, will you, please?"

She went to the console and pushed a button, "Betty? Can you come in, please? It's Florida...yes, that's right, Florida. And ask Menikov to see if we have anything on a possible merger of the Japanese people and the Chileans; it's fairly recent, but there might be something pertinent. And as a long shot, a group called the Committee for Anti-American Activities...Good."

She closed the switch, sat down again, and resumed her study of the file. Soon Betty de Haas was there, plumpish and pert and bouncing nicely under her loose cashmere sweater. The best cartographer ever to come out of Holland's famous college, she was carrying her ubiquitous roll of maps. The Colonel made the introductions and said briefly, "Florida, the Everglades."

Wagnall studied her as she fixed the maps into their rollers, reaching up with delicate fingers. She had the legs of a ballet dancer, the muscles long and taut and gleaming, a tight, tight waist that seemed to balloon out above and below—an old-fashioned hourglass of a figure—and dark; intelligent eyes. *My God, this sonofabitch Tobin's got it made* he thought. He remembered the redheaded Rena, her small, boyish figure and the sensual light on her young face, and he wondered how many more of them were tucked away in the attic or the cellars of the fine old London house.

21

Betty looked over her shoulder at him and caught him examining her body. He looked away quickly. "Would you have a note of the precise area, perhaps, Mr. Wagnall?" she asked

Wagnall nodded. "Take a line west to east from Fort Myers to Lake Worth, below the Okeechobee Lake. Due south from La Belle, and due south from Belle Glade in the southeastern extremity of the Lake. As far south as the National Park." He grimaced. "That's five or six thousand square miles of nothing but mud and mangrove and cypress swamp. But the probability is, from what Intelligence we've been able to glean, that the center of operations, so to speak, might be from Jones' Old Town as far south as a few miles from the highway to which they must have access, and probably not much more than thirty or forty miles west of Highway 27."

"Six hundred square miles, that's not very much," said the Colonel. "A hundred trained men could drive their way through that in a week, flush out anything hiding there."

"No, sit. The terrain is against us. Yes, we did that once, and we got nowhere. The Strickland found that they'd simply moved out, gone deep into the Seminole Indian Reservation thirty or forty miles to the north. That's when we turned the National Guard loose, but within a week, there was no sign of them. They'd moved south again."

"Their funds, that's the crux of the matter, isn't it? Where do they get them from?"

For a long time, Wagnall made no reply. He sipped at his Irish and said at last, "Let me answer the question behind your question. Unhappily, America's not a popular country nowadays, and I suppose there are many reasons for that. Or at least, one overriding one. All over the world, there are powerful people, wealthy people, who would like to see us...cut down to size. So any anti-American activities, even when they are as radical as this, will never want for funds. And where there's the money... it's easy to find the arms. Their last delivery—the last we know about—was a planeload of Kalashnikov submachine guns brought in from Czechoslovakia. They were originally intended for Chile, but somewhere in the Caribbean, the plane landed to refuel and took off again for Florida. Four hundred guns were dropped by parachute. Once its load was released, the plane turned due east—we had it on radar all the time. It blew up and crashed, just north of Grand Bahama Island."

"Ha!" the Colonel said, almost gleefully, "and no bits and pieces of it left for examination, I imagine?"

"On the contrary. The Coast Guard was carrying out some experimental work close by. They recovered parts of the bomb bay. There was a timing device to set off a kilo of TNT one hour after the bomb bays were opened. It was faulty. The plane crashed earlier than intended, or we'd never have known a damn thing about it."

The Colonel's eyes were gleaming. "And the plane itself?"

"An old World War II bomber, an Avro Lancaster, four props, a maximum load of fourteen thousand pounds..."

"I know all about the Avro..."

"...all its marking painted out, but we traced it to Venezuela. It had been hijacked from a military airfield outside Caracas."

Colonel Tobin said thoughtfully, "So somewhere in your angry swamps, Simon Kirby has armed a bunch of fanatics with a minimum of four hundred submachine guns. Plus, whatever he had before and whatever he's gotten hold of since." He went over and stared at the maps, brooding. Betty pulled them down for him one by one at his signal.

For a long time, nobody spoke. There was the tinkle of glass as Pamela went round with the bottle and the ice bucket. Betty de Haas said quietly, reading her Colonel's mind, "I can have every possible route *out* of that area annotated within twenty-four hours."

He nodded. "Good. Do that. I'll need Rick Meyers, Cass Fragonard, Efrem Collas, and...who else? Yes, Manuel, he should feel at home in the swamps. Where's 279 at this moment?"

Two-seven-nine was the source of the information on the voice print machine. Betty looked across at Pamela Charles; she was already at the console, throwing the switch, and she said quietly, "Movement Control, two-seven-nine, please." In a moment, the slip was fed through; she tore it off and read, "He's still in Washington, leaving for San Clemente tonight at twenty-hundred hours."

"No. Have him stand by to meet Paul in Miami, security red." The Colonel turned to Wagnall. His pale blue eyes were probing deeply. He said, "How many people know of your visit to me, Mr. Wagnall?"

Wagnall smiled slowly. "Almost nobody, Colonel. I have a letter from...a very high authority, which I am empowered to use if it becomes necessary. If you'd permit it I would prefer a certain reticence."

"Reticence?" The Colonel snorted. "Dammit, man, I *demand* reticence—it's the essence of good security. I don't suppose your esteemed President wants to get involved in this mess unless he has to, and he's perfectly right. Besides, I'll have a copy of your letter within twenty-four hours."

He didn't bother with Wagnall's look of acute shock. Instead, he said, "Very well, I'll give you my terms. Absolute authority. No interference. No word of my activities to anybody. And that includes your 'high authority.' All you have to do is go home and say the matter is in hand and will be attended to. Is that acceptable?"

"Acceptable. Should we discuss costs?"

"No, sir. My computers will send you a bill. It will be considerable."

"And that's acceptable too." Almost wistfully he asked,

24

"Could you give me a time schedule, perhaps?"

"No, sir. I will merely make you a promise. Your Simon Kirby is as good as dead. And his CAAA is going to get its arse kicked out of there. I'll deliver them for you, neatly gift-wrapped, and what you do with them then...that's your business."

Wagnall stood up. He drained his Irish and set the crystal glass down almost reluctantly. He was conscious, and almost shocked by it, that all his worries seemed instantly to have disappeared. There was an air of competence about Colonel Tobin that left him startled and perplexed; it was as though, in his secret thoughts, he could not allow anyone else the same kind of proficiency that he himself practiced so perfectly. It was almost as though, for the first time in his life, he had met a man more capable than he was. There was an aura there...

He found it alarming.

He saw Betty de Haas writing fast and furiously on her pad as she studied her beloved maps, and Pamela Charles was moving towards him, swaying, holding out her hand. He took it warily, and said, feeling foolish, "Will we meet again, Miss Charles?"

"Perhaps."

Oh, that cool, controlled look in her eyes! He looked at the Colonel, a tightly knit, wiry man with the look of a prowling animal, a leopard perhaps, and he thought to himself, *There's only one way to put it, everyone in this house is feline, ready to pounce; controlled and relaxed, but...ready.* Even the plump and bouncy little de Haas woman—there was a tension in the way she moved, as though everything were all coiled up inside her and ready to strike out.

And as for Pamela Charles...An amber light flashed and she was at the console. She took the plug, placed it in her ear, threw the switch, and listened for a while. As he stood there watching her, he saw her scribble a note quickly on a slip of paper and hand it to the Colonel.

Colonel Tobin read it and grunted. He said, very mildly, "There's one more thing, Mr. Wagnall, a trivial matter, but you may as well be kept informed. It seems there was a man watching this house from the front, and another, dammit, trying to get onto my roof. Your men, I understand, calling themselves Secret Service."

Wagnall was startled. He threw an anguished glance at Pamela Charles; her eyes were mocking him, he was sure. He looked back at the Colonel and said, "Yes, I'm afraid so. They make me travel with a couple of Secret Service men. Not my own choice, I must admit. I'm sorry they showed themselves—they're not supposed to."

"Well, they're under lock and key, both of them. I had them picked up. I don't like people prowling around my quarters."

Wagnall was smiling again, hiding his embarrassment. "Yes, of course, I understand. I hope you'll forgive me."

Tobin grunted. He pressed a switch on the console. "Roberts? You can turn those two idiots loose now. Give them back their little pistols and escort them as far as the Square. You've had no trouble with them?"

Sergeant Robert's voice was cheerful, "No, sir. They're very nice fellows, as a matter of fact. I gave them both a drink."

"Oh, dear. Not wasting the best Irish on them, I hope?"

"Oh no, sir. They drink a thing called bourbon. I sent out for some—it's terrible stuff."

"Good, that's the proper thing to do. Tell them that if they show up anywhere near my house again, I will personally break all their bloody legs for them."

"Yes, sir."

The Colonel flicked the switch back. The green light that meant the doors were now unlocked came on, and he held out his hand to Wagnall, "Well, give me a month. Will that satisfy you?"

Wagnall nodded. "I take it you'll need access to our

Intelligence reports?"

"No, I will not. They may or may not be accurate. I'd rather use my own."

"As you wish. When you wish to reach me, I have a phone number you can use..."

"I have it already."

There was a momentary silence. Then, "Oh."

He took the Colonel's hand and shook it, nearly breaking his own knuckles; and threw another look at Pamela Charles, wishing he could get to know her better. He had never seen flesh more creamy, more smooth and exciting. He saw that Betty de Haas was watching him quizzically; the urge to reach out and pat her tight little behind was almost irresistible. She held the door open for him, and he put a hand on her shoulder, saying gravely, "So nice to have met you, Miss de Haas."

Rena, the lovely young redheaded teenager was at the front door, opening it for him, and he said to himself three times in succession: "My God, my God, my God..."

She closed the door behind him and he thought that London was the greatest city in the world.

Inside the huge study, the Colonel sighed. "My God, we're going to America," he said: "I never thought it could happen." He frowned at the maps. "Betty, every possible way in and out—I want every inch of that territory mapped. It's not going to be easy. What have we got?"

"The satellite maps from the Institute, the American Defense Department maps, the old Spanish charts which were remarkably thorough for their time, and some very good charts from the U.S. Natural History Foundation. It should be enough. There might be a few surprises when you get there."

"Uh-huh. So get to it. I want it in a hurry."

"All right." He patted her breast affectionately. She rolled up the sheaf of maps, tucked them under her arm, and went up to her green and white rooms in the attic to start on the research, the annotations, the calculations.

The Colonel looked at Pamela Charles. He rubbed his taut stomach, wondering if he were getting a little flabby there; it was like a sheet of carbon steel. He said brusquely, "Give me a massage, Charles, will you? A good rub down, and then we'll make love. I feel restless."

"All right. I'll get the things."

She pulled down the leather topped strip couch from its walnut cabinet in the wall, set out the alcohol and the powder and the vibrator, and went off to change her clothes. The Colonel stripped down to the skin and lay down on his back, waiting for her, staring up at the ornate, old-fashioned ceiling, counting the curlicues and wondering about a man called Simon Kirby who killed off his own pilots just in case they might get captured and talk.

When she came back, she was wearing her short Black kimono, her long legs pale and smooth as alabaster, her hair hanging down over her shoulders now in the fashion he liked so much.

He closed his eyes and let her go to work on him.

He opened them once, slid a hand gently along her rump, and said, "Rick Meyers and the others?"

Her voice was very low. Her hands were soft and skillful. "They'll be here at eight-thirty. I arranged dinner for them."

"Good. What about Paul?"

"Paul's due in at midnight. Did you remember about Rena?"

"Ah yes, Rena. She wants to go out into the field. Do you think she's ready?"

"Yes, I would say so."

"She's rather young, you know. Bright, alert, pretty...But very young."

Momentarily, the hands had stopped moving, "Pretty? Yes, I suppose she is. A little skinny...But she's ready—Betty's sure of it, and so am I." The hands were moving again, caressing.

The Colonel said, "I wonder...Let's see what Rick has to say. No, he doesn't know her well enough yet. Does she realize that she has a very good chance of getting killed off?"

"She knows it. But it's a diminished chance if she's with Rick, wouldn't you say?"

"She seems so fragile."

"She's a lot tougher than she looks. She passed all the exams with flying colors, all of them, even the physical."

"Ah yes, the physical, I should have been there." The hands stopped again, briefly, then moved on. The Colonel said at last, his mind not quite made up, "Let her join the dinner tonight for a briefing. Can we really expose her to this kind of danger?"

"We can try."

"That's not what I meant. Is she tough enough for that?"

Pamela Charles shrugged. "There's a lot more to that chick than meets the eye. Yes, I'd say she's tough enough. But there's really only one way to find out, isn't there?"

"You're a very coldhearted woman, Charles, aren't you?"

"No, sir. I just calculate well." The touch of her hands was ecstasy.

All right, remind me to speak to Rick about it tonight. It might not be easy, at that."

"If there's a way to do it, Rick Meyers will find it."

"Yes, you're right, of course."

"I'm always right."

His hand, hard and calloused and yet gentle, was cupping her breast, the nipple between his fingers; he never ceased to wonder at the firm resilience of it. "Now," he said.

She slipped off her robe and lay down beside him.

CHAPTER 3

Frogleg Creek.

Coordinates: 81.06E
         26.12N

Rick Meyers thought he had never seen a more alarming place.

There was an ancient heritage that ran through his blood, and his first thought was of atavism; it was fears such as these that had driven the most remote of his ancestors onto dry land, out of the swamps.

The long, groping roots of the mangroves seemed to have a will of their own, as though all the old demons were still at work, and even the shrill cacophony of the frogs and the crickets and the birds seemed to hold a threat of its own. He felt as though he were invading a territory in which he was not welcome.

He was a slight, dark-visaged man with a restless, inquiring air about him, his sharply pointed nose always turning this way and that, his eyes constantly moving. He was quiet, methodical, and always sure that what he was doing was right, because he never did anything at all until he *knew* it was, right. He was a historian, a man with a marvelously uncluttered mind, full of recondite information that, tucked away at the back of his brain, might one day come in useful; and he had made the study and practice of Intelligence his life's work.

The map, skillfully drawn in the most minute detail, was etched onto his khaki-colored handkerchief, invisible. He soaked it in the slimy water, laid it out on the moss, and watching the colored lines appear, said in a very low voice, "It's hard to tell. We've covered, what, three miles? Since we left the inlet?"

She nodded. She wore torn jeans now and a cotton tank-top, and her red hair was grimy with the swamp's black waters. She grimaced and said, "My God, I even smell. Yes, I'd say three miles, a little more."

He was pleased; it was three and one-quarter miles exactly by his own careful reckoning. Pleased, because it dispelled another of his doubts. Betty had pleaded, "Take her, Rick, she's bright," and he had said, "Too young, far too young."

There'd almost been a quarrel, but not quite. The Colonel had said quietly, "I won't order it, Rick, she's on your staff, you have to approve. But Betty's right, she'll be worth her weight in gold to you."

Well, an attractive companion at least, he had thought and had given way. He touched a grimy finger to the map—one of Betty's unexpected maps. "Here, then, this is where we are now. The house should be just ahead of us, half a mile, no more. Are you all right?"

Rena Susac laughed. She shook the long, lank hair away from her face and said, "Yes, of course, why shouldn't I be?" She was just a kid, twenty-three years old last month, and only two years in Colonel Tobin's Private Army. She came from Yugoslavia, from Dubrovnik, and there was an offshore island named after her family. Her English was accented, a strange and intriguing lilt to it. She said again, "Yes, I'm all right. Wherever you can go, I can. And for just as long."

"I doubt that." He smiled. "I hope you'll never have to keep up with me." Not conscious of changing the subject, he

31

said, "I can hear running water."

They struggled through the morass together and found a small clearing where there was indeed a fast-running stream of clear water. She looked at the little compass and said, "We changed course by five degrees, for two hundred and fifty yards. What happens if we lose the compass?"

"We don't. But if we do, we head due west, hit the beach again, start over—another fifteen hours of all this." He studied the map again, thought about it, and said, "If we followed the stream south, we should get to the house, or whatever it is, in about half an hour. If you're tired, we can rest up nearby for a while."

"Okay. Can we make a fire?"

"No fires."

"I just thought I'd make you a beef Stroganoff." She studied his dark, brooding eyes for a moment. "Betty had the idea you didn't really want me along on this trip. Is that right?"

"Nope."

"I wish you'd tell me."

He could sense that she was perturbed about it, and he shook his head. "No, it's just not true that I didn't want you. I was afraid you might not be up to it. There's a difference. If the choice had been mine, I'd have looked for someone...older, maybe. Tougher, anyway."

"I'm plenty tough when I have to be."

"But you have to run at the first sign of trouble. The Colonel's own orders."

"But he left it up to me to decide where the trouble was insuperable or not."

"Yes. Just don't sell them short, these bastards. They don't play games." He hesitated, wondering if he should tell her, and then decided to drive the point home. "Strickland's last attempt, before they got pulled out, was to send a detachment of his men to the area just south of us. They found four bodies tied to a tree, strangled by wire round their necks. One of them was a woman."

"A woman who didn't know when to run. You're not scaring me."

"They'd sent him a note telling him where to find the bodies. What they didn't tell him was that they'd booby-trapped the place. Oh, Strickland's a bright man—he was ready for that. He found seven land mines set for him and managed to defuse them all." He sighed. "There was one more, under the girl's body, and that's the one they didn't find till it was too late. Three men killed, four wounded. They'd slipped it down here between her thighs, up tight...A dead woman, can you believe that? So don't ever think that..."

There was a certain look in her green eyes, and her hand was on his arm. He swung round and saw, through the dense shrubbery that was all around them, a silently gliding canoe. She had already slithered to the ground, forcing her skinny little body into the moss, and he lay close beside her and watched as the canoe went by, a dugout with four men in it. One man in the stern was punting it along, and the others, seated forward, all carried machine pistols; one of them had a string of hand grenades around his belt, and they were less than sixty feet away.

She had the little Mino camera out, its shutter silenced by Edgars Jefferson's marvelously skilled experts. When the boat had gone, he whispered, "Any good?"

She nodded. "Two good pictures, three possibles. And does that mean we're in the middle of them?"

"No. It just means we're in their territory, and we already knew that. We'll wait. There may be others."

Quietly they pulled deeper under the bushes. A small snake was close beside her, and as they both watched, it slithered up over her thigh; she did not move. It raised its tiny head and looked at her, the tongue darting, and she held her breath. Behind him, Rick was groping for a stick. Not finding one quickly

33

enough, he struck out suddenly, a movement so fast she hardly saw it, and struck at it with the flat of his hand, just below the head. It went flying into the water.

"A krait," he whispered.

"No, a moccasin. It's just as deadly." She laughed, a short, silent laugh of relief, and he saw her shudder. He reached out to touch her; letting his hand rest on her thigh, taut under the denim.

They waited for half an hour, and there were no more dugouts. They moved on south, walking in the ankle-deep water close to the banks, letting the trailing festoons of moss hide their presence. He walked ahead with the big pack on his back, and she followed a few paces behind with their rolled-up blankets and the compass, checking their course every hundred yards and keeping a mental note of the mean direction.

Soon he stopped and crouched down on his heels. Looking back at her, he saw that she had taken cover too, and when he pointed, she crept up to him and watched. The house was there, just where Betty had said it would be.

But not a house; a houseboat.

He knew her report almost by heart:

"The aerial photographs show a small and possibly seldom used wharf with a fairly well defined path back among the overhanging trees where there must be a dwelling of some sort, probably an alligator-hunter's shack. A bundle of alligator skins on board a small wooden boat is clearly visible on one of the pictures. This stream, however (which is presumably a spring), begins and ends nowhere, and cannot therefore be used for much in the way of commerce. There are other photographs which show larger quantities of skins being loaded at a path that meets the stream three point seven miles to the southeast, coordinates 471-398 on Map 22, and there is probably an overland route running parallel with the stream, since there are signs of porterage at several points. The area is scarcely traveled at all. Whoever lives in the house (if it is occupied at present), is a homebody. This is well into the area in which reports indicate the CAAA is operating, and the greatest caution should therefore be exercised at all times. It is possible that this house is, or has been, used by the CAAA, since it lies on the main route between two points where we know they have been..."

They waited a long time, listening and watching. There was no sound, no movement. He said at last, "I can smell food being cooked." She nodded and whispered, "Tomatoes frying."

"All right. I'm going in. You know what you have to do?"

"I know."

"If a shot is fired, you run." He touched her face lightly and said: "You *run*, Rena. You clear out. No heroics at all. You understand?"

"Why don't I go in, and you do the running?"

He sighed, taking the P38 from his belt and giving it to her. He gave her the map too, and hid the backpack under the bushes. "Well, here goes," he whispered. "You stay here, whatever happens. Unless there's shooting, and then..."

She looked charming, sitting there patiently and nodding her head in resignation, as though Papa were giving her a lesson she'd already learned by heart. Her teeth were shining, her eyes bright, and she said, "Rick, you poor dear, you do run on, don't you?"

"It's the father-daughter idea...And I wonder if that could be construed as an incestuous thought? I suppose it could."

"Not yet, anyway," she countered.

He laughed softly. He moved off, a snake himself now, slithering forward on his belly and making no sound at all. He got within twenty yards of the houseboat and then detoured more deeply into the swamp, crawling around it on three sides, sometimes up to his neck in slime, sometimes forcing his thin body through the tightly confining mangrove roots. He climbed a tree and watched for half an hour, and saw nothing and heard nothing, but there was the constant smell of the food, burning now. He climbed down, knowing that country people, poor people, did not easily burn their food without some reason, and that reason *could* be...The cook had evidently left the kitchen, not even going back to turn down the flame, and the logical explanation was that Rick had been discovered. He stood up, showing himself, carefully not moving too fast and keeping his hands well away from his pockets. He was changing his cover story quickly, to fit the new circumstances. The new story would permit him to prowl around like this and still appear innocent. Suddenly he saw him, an old, old man, so ancient as to be a parchment skin over a skeleton, and the old man was moving out from under cover with a shotgun leveled at his head.

The face was the face of a dead man, a stringy white beard and sunken cheeks, but the eyes seemed to be on fire, almost laughing now. The gun was rock-steady. Rick Meyers stood still and raised his hands.

The old man said, "I seen you, Spaniard. I seen you all the time. You come from General Galvez?"

"Galvez?" He was startled. He knew already. There was a reason for that strange light in the eyes. He said gently, "Galvez is dead, old man."

"Yeah, that's what they tell me. Don't mean I believe it none, though."

"General Galvez? There's been no General Galvez around these parts for two hundred years."

"Hurricane blew his boats into the Bay—he took off up Shark River—he's still prowling around some place, and don't you try to fool me, Spaniard, How come you ain't wearing your armor? You supposed to have a helmet on your head, all shined up so's we kin take a bead on it...You another o' them deserters, Spaniard?"

Rick sighed, patient with the old man's madness. He said gently, "No Spaniard, old man. I'm not here to harm you."

"Only Spaniards got cause to hide around my place, they all know that. You ain't a Spaniard, how come you're hiding? I seen you creeping around."

"Somebody took a couple of shots at me back there, I was scared."

"Yeah? How come I didn't hear no shooting? I got good ears."

"A long way back. I still wanted to be sure."

The old man lowered his shotgun, and as Rick put down his bands, he said sharply, "No! You keep them hands where I kin see 'em. You got another gun aimed right at your liver—we gonna eat it tonight, you ain't careful. There."

He jerked his head, and Rick turned and saw a young woman in rags, standing half behind him. She was barefoot and grimy, a *Tobacco Road* young woman who held her rusting shotgun steadily and looked him up and down with a kind of startled innocence. He wondered how old she might be. Twenty, perhaps? Her body was full, an animal ripeness, her legs muscular and sturdy, and the dress was an old shift that barely covered her. But it was her eyes that fascinated him; they were cold gray and large and round, and somehow...expectant. She was fully matured, but still a child, a creature who was as much a part of the swamp as the black mud that clung to her feet. He was startled to realize that the mere sight of her moved him deeply, a sensuality that somehow got to him in spite of all the logic he lived by. Was it the look in those astonishing eyes? Or the naked body under that piece of rag? She disturbed him, moved him, excited him.

"You alone, Spaniard?" the old man asked.

Rick shook his head. "No. I've got a girl with me."

The child-woman nodded. "He's right, granpaw. I seen her. Back there a ways, hiding under the bushes, looks like she's scared too."

"And I'm no Spaniard, I keep telling you."

"All right, what are you then? You tell me that, maybe I let you go, if'n I believe you."

"I'm a trader. I'm looking for alligator skins."

"You don't look like no trader to me..." The old man broke off and said, "Well, maybe you do at that, you got the same shifty look in your eyes. You want to buy skins? I got seven, eight, stashed away. They ain't been cured none they smell a mite—but good skins. How much you aim to pay?"

"Twenty cents a foot."

"Twenty cents, eh?" He rubbed a hand over his chin and turned to the girl. "How much we get last time, Melanie?"

"Twenty-seven."

"Then you got to go higher'n that, Spaniard. Else you don't git a mean one o' my skins."

Did he believe him? Perhaps not, Rick thought. He took a chance and said, "Why don't we go into the house and sit down and talk? You think that's a good idea?"

The skeleton shook its head; Rick wondered why he could not hear the bones rattling. But the young girl laughed suddenly and said; "Why not, granpaw? Sarah's got herself the gun too. If'n he tries anything sassy, she's like to blow his head clean off. Flagstaff's around some place too, and you know Flagstaff, he's got a bead on him too for sure, right between them lovely black eyes."

The old man was scratching at the insects around his groin. "What we got to talk about, Spaniard?"

Rick hesitated. "Money? I need some information."

"I git along fine without money—I don't need none. Well, maybe that ain't exactly true; them bastids took away my best gun, threw it out in the swamp someplace?"

"What bastards are they?"

"Bastids. Who's the girl back there?"

"Just a girl. She helps me."

The young woman said: "Kinda skinny, granpaw. She's got red hair, I mean real red."

The old man thought hard, squinting, fingering his pallid cheeks. "How much money you got?"

"Enough."

He thought again for a while. The girl was already moving towards the ramshackle houseboat, gesturing. Rick turned his back on the old man and went with her. "You don't have to be afraid, Melanie," he said gently. "Neither of you."

"Afraid?" She turned and laughed again, a laugh of genuine amusement, then turned back and moved on, across the flimsy board that lay between the boat and the land. There were bundles of dried alligator skins on the deck, salted down and wrapped in burlap, and there were sacks of salt nearby.

The cabin was wide and airy, painted long ago with white distemper that was now flaking off everywhere. There was a bare plank table and a single, overstuffed armchair of the kind that can be seen rotting on any garbage dump, with a plank cupboard and a plank bench running down one side of the room. On the other side, two brass bedsteads were covered over with a motley selection of blankets. The air was thick with the scent of cooking, and there was greasy smoke coming from the galley that lay forward of the cabin. The old man came in behind them and said, not caring much about it, "You done burned them tomatoes agin."

Rick sat down on the bursting armchair, its brilliant red faded now and horribly stained. Taking the silver flask from his pocket, he handed it silently to his host. The old man tossed his gun carelessly onto one of the beds, picked up the flask, and examined it. Rick wondered if he'd ever get back again; it was a much prized possession, a present from the Colonel—full of the

Colonel's private stock of Irish. The old man eased off the
screw-top, took a few sips, and thought about it for a long time.
Then he nodded appreciatively, put the flask to his lips, and
drained it dry. He ran a thin, white hand over his mouth, took a
long breath, squinted at Rick; and said, "You got any more of
that stuff, Spaniard?"

Rick nodded. "Not here. But there's plenty more where
that came from."

"Two, three bottles of that stuff, you got all the
information you need. You don't have to talk about money
none."

"All right. You've got a deal."

"Yeah. How'm I gonna trust you to deliver?"

Unexpectedly, the young woman said gravely, "You can
trust him, granpaw."

The old man looked at her and said, puzzled; "You sure
about that?"

"I'm sure." She too had tossed her gun onto the bed.

Rick noticed that the safety catches on both of them were
off, and he sighed. "Tell me your name, old man. Mine's Rick
Meyers."

"My name?" He plucked at his beard, his eyes screwed
up. "I don't have no name."

"Old Man, that's his name," Melanie said.

"And yours is Melanie. Who's Sarah?"

"Sarah's my sister."

"And Flagstaff?"

She laughed. She was always laughing, this girl, quite
unexpectedly finding amusement where no cause for it seemed to
exist. It seemed to light up her grubby face. She plunked herself
down on the bed by the guns, sitting cross-legged and pulling the
ragged gray dress down between her naked thighs, hiding the
hair there and bouncing up and down on the creaking springs.
There was nothing at all under the dress, a shift carelessly hiding

40

most of her body. Her breasts were full, too full, and they jiggled when she moved. "You think I'm pretty?" she asked.

He nodded. "Yes, you're pretty. Who's Flagstaff?"

"Flagstaff's an Indian—he don't count for nothing. He just hangs around here so he can get into bed with me or Sarah when he thinks the old man ain't looking."

The old man was laughing now too, throwing back his head and slapping his thigh, and Melanie said, "Only the old man knows everything there is to know, don't you, granpaw?"

He was spluttering, his toothless mouth a dark red gap in a gray parchment face, and he said happily, "In these parts, Spaniard, there ain't much to make a young girl happy, only Flagstaff."

"And where is he now?"

Melanie shrugged. "Out there someplace, up in one of them trees, most likely. That's where he likes to set all day, when he ain't shooting gators. And he can put a bullet through a gator's eye so far off you can't even see it."

"A Seminole?"

"I guess. Ain't no other kind of Indian around here none."

Rick wondered how Rena was faring out there, with Sarah watching her and a Seminole up in the branches of his favorite mangrove. "He's not likely to harm my girl, is he?"

Melanie shook her head. She said gravely, "Not excepting Old Man will tell him to." She stood up abruptly, sliding her naked haunches off the bed. Running to the entrance, she put her fingers to her lips and whistled shrilly. When she turned back, she was laughing again, rubbing her hands over her breasts and saying, "You really think I'm pretty? For sure?"

She stood there like a raggedy doll, her bare feet spread wide on the plank floor, her legs solid, the dress tight over her hips and bust, gaping wide in the center. He threw a quick look at the old man, grinning at him now, nodded, and said, "Yes, I think you're very pretty."

41

"You want to get there, in between my legs, it's okay with me."

The urge to take her at her word was almost insuperable; it shocked him, and he wondered if it was the effect of the swamp, the old atavistic urges bursting through the patina of civilization. "It's not really the time, Melanie."

"I seen you looking. Don't think I didn't see you."

"Just a reflex action."

"Huh?"

He sighed. She flopped onto the bed again, and lay down on her belly, one hand trailing on the floor, her tangled, grubby hair resting on the butt of the shotgun. She was laughing again. Just then the boat rocked gently and there was a shadow at the entrance, and another young girl was there. Much younger than Melanie, fifteen or sixteen, perhaps, she was dressed in the same raggedy kind of shift, a bright-eyed child with long, straggly hair that came down to her waist. She too was barefoot, and she too carried an ancient shotgun, its barrel horribly rusted, its stock chipped and cracked. She carried it carelessly, a finger hooked around the trigger guard; and she stood there, her weight on one leg, the other crooked at the knee; and stared at him.

Melanie said carelessly, "That's Sarah—she's my sister—she ain't more'n fifteen years old maybe. You want her too, you can have her. Only, don't let Flagstaff see you. He's real hot for her—he's like to get real mad."

The old man had stopped laughing. He was staring thoughtfully at the floor, puzzling something out, and he said suddenly, "When you gonna get me my whiskey, Spaniard?"

Rick could not take his eyes off the young girl. Her eyes were wide and solemn and gray, and there was a downward tilt to the edges of the full and petulant mouth. The hair hung down, long and enticing, and there was a rip in her dress at the waist, exposing the edge of a pelvic bone. She had not taken her grave eyes off him.

He said quickly, "Soon, Old Man. Very soon. Tell me about the strangers in the swamp."

The old man's eyes were burning through him, "Strangers?"

"Yes. A lot of people around who don't belong here. You must know about them."

The old man was not laughing any more. He threw an anguished look at Melanie. She too was no longer smiling. The old man said at last, "Why you want to know about them, Spaniard? They ain't nothing but trash. Foreign trash."

"Then you've seen them."

"Sure I seen 'em, ain't nothing moves in this swamp I don't see."

"Close by? Are there any of them near here?"

There was an angry look on his face. He said, "They come, they go, them bastids."

"When was the last time you saw them?"

"Bastids. Last time was...Oh, I don't know when that was."

"Yesterday, granpaw, that was when they hit you," Melanie reminded him.

"Yesterday? Seems longer'n that...One of them punched me in the gut, made me real sick. What did they want to do that for? I wasn't harming them none. They took away my best gun—didn't know got four, five more hidden away. How'm I gonna shoot them gators without a gun, kin you tell me that?"

"Will you tell me everything you know about them, Old Man?"

There was a long, long silence. The old man began drumming on his knee with his bony fingers. At last he stood up and went to the bed where Melanie was, pulled the shotgun from under her, and said, looking back over a gaunt shoulder, "How many bottles o' that whiskey you aim to pass onto me?"

"Six, a dozen, as much as you want."

"How soon can I start tastin'?"

"As soon as possible. Today, tomorrow."

He thought for a while, "You make that stuff yourself? That's pretty good sippin' whiskey."

"The best there is."

The old man pulled at his earlobe and stood there, reflecting. He said to Melanie, gruffly, "You tell him, you tell him what he wants to know. I aim to eat my dinner."

He stalked into the kitchen, came out with a pot of burned food in an old iron casserole, and went out. The boat rocked slightly as he stepped over the long plank and onto the shore and disappeared into the swamp.

Melanie patted the bed beside her and said softly, "You come set close by me, where I kip git my hands on you if'n I want. You give me what I want, I give you what you want, so you come set closer to me."

He looked at Sarah. She had neither moved nor spoken, nor had she taken her solemn eyes off him.

He sat by Melanie and put a hand on her naked rump under the flimsy dress, scratching her smooth flesh lightly with his fingernails.

Sarah was still watching.

Rena Susac was still there where he had left her when, two hours later, Rick Meyers struggled through the marsh weeds back to her hiding place. He felt guilty.

He sat down beside her. "The people in the houseboat have been working with some of the CAAA, showing them the tracks through the swamp. But they fell out..."

"That's good. You don't seem very happy about it."

He said, worrying about it, "They exacted a price, and I found I was happy to pay it."

She was puzzled, her shrewd eyes on him, wondering.

Her red hair was shining now, washed out in the stream, clinging to her wetly. She said quietly, "And a young girl was watching us, but she went away a couple of hours ago?"

"Yes, I know. Her name is Sarah. There's another one, a little older, whose name's Melanie. And there's an old, old man, a skeleton, whose name is...Old Man. And an Indian named Flagstaff who's out here somewhere, watching you all the time."

"Behind you." She was smiling at him. "Directly behind you, up in the branches of a mangrove tree. I spotted him an hour ago, and he hasn't moved once, not a muscle."

"He's a Seminole. It seems he just turned up one day, and decided to stay. With good reason." He sighed. "He's part of the family now, a silent, irremovable part of the household."

"What did you find out?"

"A great deal. They're building redoubts all over the swamp, haphazardly it seems, though I don't really believe that. We'll know more later. They've been bringing in great slabs of timber, dumping them here and there and everywhere, it can only mean redoubts, strongpoints."

"You said they fell out..."

"Yes. I gathered that it was...a pretty cozy arrangement, but one of them, and it must have been Kirby himself—a black patch over his eye—beat up the old man for no reason at all, to discipline him, they said. And in a family like that...There's a love there among the three of them that's quite remarkable. And a hatred, therefore, for Kirby and his men. Yes, it's good."

He had not moved. "This Indian, up in the tree. Can I get a look at him from here?"

"No, from further down the stream. He's shout thirty, lean, tough-looking, tall, very dark, thick black hair, black eyes, thin nose, high forehead, wears blue jeans and a green tartan shirt, a knife in his belt, and a very fancy rifle across his knees."

Rick said sharply, "A *fancy* rifle? Could it be a Kalashnikov?"

45

"It *is* a Kalashnikov. You can't mistake them."

"Well, that's very interesting."

"Yes, I thought you'd like that bit." She was mocking him again, and she said, "What sort of inference does Intelligence derive from that?"

"None. We tuck the information away at the backs of our minds, for future reference if necessary."

"If they gave it to him, it might mean he's on their side."

"What *might* be meant doesn't count. Don't try to be too smart. It's more probable that he stole it from them."

"Oh. Well, I was only trying."

He stood up and pulled her to her feet, and said lightly, "Nothing worse than a trying child." He was smiling at her, but she said, frowning, "What's she like, this...Melanie? The other one looked a bit...animal."

"Perhaps that's the right word for both of them. Shall we go?"

He shouldered the big bundle, and they moved off together, in silence. Slowly the darkness of the swamp closed in on them.

CHAPTER 4

Santasville.

Coordinates: 80.92E
                        26.72N

Simon Kirby sat at the window, staring out through the half-closed drapes at the long gray ribbon of Highway 41. Close beside it, the Tamiami Canal ran straight as a die, due east.

His face was weather-beaten, scarred, deeply lined and angry, and the black patch over his left eye gave him a faintly piratical, not-of-this-century look. He still wore his jungle boots and the faded denims, but he was naked to the waist; the air conditioning in this grubby little motel was not functioning, and his chest, lean and taut and whip-corded, was streaked with perspiration.

Behind him, at the plastic-topped table, Carolyne Southby was taking down the notes he was giving her, her pencil poised, her yellow legal tablet already covered with her large, immature letters. She was a plumpish young woman of twenty-five, quite attractive in a sullen sort of way, with longish black hair and a very white skin; she had a habit of tossing the hair back from her face from time to time, a nervous reflex. She wore gold-rimmed granny glasses and a gold chain with a heavy ceramic pendant on it, a flat disk on which was incised the legend, *Change Now*. Her

47

tie-dyed shirt was open at the front, so that the shiny pottery tablet rested between her breasts, cool to her flesh, and her sleeves were rolled to the elbow. She had kicked off her sandals and was scratching at one foot with the toe of the other.

Kirby was speaking. "...and I want Kinono and twelve of his men to hit the following post offices tomorrow morning: Edgeville, Parmalee, and Verna, all on Highway 70; Park Ridge, Avon Park, and Lake Placid, all on Highway 27; Kenansville, Lokosee, and Osoway on 441. Also the Cyprus Knee Museum in Palmdale. The standard packaged high explosive, except at the museum. He can try out the new plastic there, exactly one-and-a-half pounds of it, and I want photographs taken immediately after the explosion, and a fully detailed report submitted within six hours—extent of the destruction, and so forth. What time is it?"

She looked at her watch, "Three-forty, another twenty minutes."

He grunted. He could net control his impatience, and she said, frowning, "It's not going to work, you know. He should be using a bomb, the one weapon you can't argue with."

"Yes, I know. But this is...a bonus. My God, if it comes off..."

"I don't think it will, Simon. I have a feeling about it."

"Out of the blue...it just might."

She shook her head, tossing back the hair. "You don't kill a President on the spur of the moment. It takes months of planning. Months."

"And the essence of good tactics is to seize an opportunity when it shows itself. Don't try and teach me my business, you stupid bitch."

She laughed shortly and swung round to look at him.

"A bitch, maybe. Stupid? No."

He said, "Twenty minutes, for Chrissake. Instructions to Joe and Harry. Letter bombs to the next twenty people listed, all to be sent from over the state line, somewhere in Georgia, maybe

Brunswick. For Carlos Santina, there's a Cuban demo starting up on Friday in Delray Beach. I want him there to get the feel of it, see if he can maybe start trouble. He'd better take a few men with him, and I want at least one sniper, at least one dead pig. Draw a check on the Geneva account, to the order of Consolidated Interfield Arms, one hundred thousand dollars even, have Ahmed Sarat deliver it by hand, personally. Have Groups Six, Nine, and Fourteen moved back, to Point Baker, that's where we'll be tomorrow. I want to take a look at those guns. That's it. Have I got time for a shower?"

She checked her watch again: "Twelve minutes."

He went into the bathroom, and she heard the shower running as she tore out the top four sheets of her pad and locked them safely away in the suitcase. While she waited, she took out a small, pencil-shaped detonator and stripped it down carefully, closing her eyes and fingering the delicate mechanism with the tips of her fingers, keeping her expert hand on it. He came back in a few minutes with a bath towel around his waist, put a casual hand on her breast and grunted at her when she pushed it, just as casually, away.

He said, "Nervous tension, that's all it is, you know, the big moment coming up, all that jazz. You're too fat for me, baby. Juicy, but too fat. All the same..."

He moved behind her and put a strong arm around her waist, holding her tight, cupping his other hand over her breast again, liking the touch of her skin. She did not struggle. She let his hand explore her, dropping down over her rounded stomach and on down to the groin; his watch caught under her belt, and he twisted his wrist round, his hand between her thighs now, then back to the plump breast, molding it.

She said, quite unmoved, "The news will be on in three minutes, so take your fucking hands off me." He let her go, switched on the T.V. set, and waited, sitting on the edge of the bed and watching a commercial without seeing it.

"That sonofabitch Strickland," Kirby said suddenly.

"What's he done now?"

"Marella came when you were out. Strickland's been pulled off, and he doesn't know why."

"Who doesn't know? Strickland or Marella?"

"Marella. If Strickland knows, he's keeping his trap shut. I don't like it. I think we're going to have to do something about it."

She was frowning, taking off her glasses and polishing them. "It can only mean one thing," she said: "The CIA's taking over, and they want him out of their hair."

"Maybe."

"What other reason could there be?"

"His own goddam incompetence."

"No. He's a good cop, if there ever was such an animal. He knows his job. No one's going to call him incompetent."

"A question of degree, isn't it? If they've got a better man up their sleeve? Marella says Strickland's pretty mad, but keeping mum about it. Only I figure..." He broke off, removed the towel, and rubbed the sweat on his chest. "These goddam motels...I figure we ought to pick up Strickland's wife. What do you think about that?"

"You think he'll have told her?"

He laughed. "A middle-class American slob, yes, he will have told her. And she can tell us. We pick her up, take her out to the swamp someplace; cut her face up a little bit, hear what she has to say, and then slice her throat open. Maybe we should send her eyeballs back to the nice Captain, let him know what we really think of him. Does that sound like a good idea to you?"

"Sure. It makes sense."

"What time is Descartes showing?"

"Six o'clock. He's switching the cars."

"Put him onto it. Have him take her over to Point Four. I want to talk to her myself."

50

She nodded. The endless commercials came to their end, and Cronkite was there, severe and dignified and slightly disapproving:

"...and here are the highlights of the news to this hour. A Secret Service man attached to the President's entourage has died after eating a sandwich heavily impregnated with poison. He has been identified as Johnny Marcangeli of Orlando, Florida. At this moment, it is not known whether or not this tragedy might be construed as an attempt on the President's life, and the White House has imposed a strict blackout on all news related to the incident. Mr. Marcangeli was taken ill during an unscheduled and unexpected stop at an Italian celebration of the Feast of La Madonna di Monde Virgine, and was rushed to Saint Michael's Hospital. He was pronounced dead on arrival. The cause of death was apparently a massive dose of a poison derived from the fungus amanita phalloides, a fairly common and highly toxic fungus which is sometimes called the Death Angel. A spokesman stated there is at least a possibility that the fungus was mistakenly believed to be an ordinary mushroom, which could have found its way into the proffered food, but at this hour we have very little information to go on. Mr. Marcangeli was twenty-seven years old. The President has sent a message of condolence to the dead man's wife, and the tour is continuing. In Southeast Asia, yet another attempt is being made to bring the new strong man to the conference table with..."

"Shit!" Simon Kirby put his fist through the T.V. screen, shattering it and lacerating the fingers of his right hand.

He was waiting for her to say "I told you so," but she kept quiet. Instead, she tore a piece from the bedsheet, slipped the glasses down to the end of her nose, and bandaged his hand for him. She said mildly, "You can get hurt doing that—a lot of voltage in a T.V. set." There was splintered glass all over the floor. She put on her sandals and tossed his boots and trousers to him.

Kirby stared morosely at her and asked, "When do we get a report?"

She shrugged. "Buzz won't be back till tomorrow afternoon. It's too hot to use the wires. We'll know then." Then she said it. "I told you he should have used a bomb. It's easy enough to imagine what happened."

It was all very simple.

News had come to the presidential cavalcade of the fiesta going on in the orange grove, and it had made a detour to shake hands and laugh and maybe drink a token glass of Chianti.

And Buzz Friendly was there.

For two days now, he had been stalking the entourage, calmly waiting for what Kirby would have called a target of opportunity. Buzz Friendly, a young radical with a penchant for experiment and a degree in forensic medicine from Berkeley; his thesis had been on the use of poison as a weapon in revolutionary history.

Someone, amid all the laughing and the joking, had passed to the President, hand over hand over hand, not a sandwich but a thick and greasy slice of pizza, wrapped in a white paper napkin and decorated with a miniature Italian flag. There had been a lot of cheering, and someone was shouting noisily as he poured a glass of homemade red wine. The President had whispered to an aide, "Hell, this isn't an election year. I don't have to eat that crap, do I?"

The aide, beaming and back-slapping, had taken it and somehow contrived to pass it on down the line. Johnny Marcangeli, hastily pulled out of his local desk job when the decision had been made to visit the fiesta, had eaten the pizza. It was three-forty in the afternoon and it was the first bite he had taken all day. It was also to be his last. The stomach pumps did their work, but the doctors were too late to save his life.

The *amanita phalloides*, as any student of forensic medicine knows, is just too fast, and too deadly.

The target of opportunity, chanced upon fortuitously, had failed; perhaps there would be other opportunities. Buzz Friendly would stay with the tour, his eyes open and, this time, a bomb handy.

"Christ, he won't even eat an ethnic hot dog," Kirby said.

"Bombs, the only answer," she repeated. "You blow something up, there's no mistake. The wrong people get killed, but that doesn't matter, because the explosion itself is...symbolical. It teaches people that you have to tear down before you can start building up a decent society. You blow up the crap and build something worthwhile...Christ, a fucking salami sandwich. It makes us all look like a bunch of amateurs."

"It was pizza." He sighed. "A bonus, that's all it would have been. A big one, the biggest yet, but..." She was tossing back her hair again, and the gesture fascinated him. He looked around the motel room, hating it, hating the blue plastic headboard and the sickly green carpeting, hating the print on the wall and the color of the draperies, hating the dripping faucet in the shower and the vinyl-covered armchair. "We'll leave a timer here and blow this place sky-high when we leave. Set it for midnight—get the bastards out of their beds. What time are you contacting the Japs?"

"Kinono's standing by from six-thirty onwards, half an hour after we leave. We'll stop somewhere down the road and arrange a meeting."

"Thank God for the Japs; we'd be out of business without

them."

She agreed. The Japanese contingent was their most efficient one. They were the men—and women—she could really empathize with. They were ruthless, skilled, and fast. In six months, working always within the tight control of Kirby's rigid orders, they had committed eighteen murders, destroyed four banks, three police stations, and the massive, gray stone building that housed Florida's Center for Governmental Studies. They had stolen a hundred and eighty-four rifles and two hundred cases of grenades from the National Guard Armory, and had hijacked one government aircraft, negotiating the release of its passengers (after which they had destroyed the plane with a time bomb) in exchange for half a million dollars.

They kept to themselves always, the Japanese; they had fallen out with the Chileans with whom they had come here, but were still correct and courteous with them; they believed the Chileans were too soft, too afraid to die, too self-centered. They kept to their own strongpoint in the swamp and came to Kirby from time to time for approval of their own plans. They could be relied upon to leave a trail of mayhem and bloodshed wherever they went.

She was crouched on the floor, picking up slivers of glass and placing them in the trash basket. He stared at her morosely. "It's a long time till six o'clock, baby."

She did not answer, knowing what was on his mind, and in a moment he said, "How long's Harry Dewitt been gone?"

"Two weeks—you know that."

"When's he due back?"

"Three days—you know that, too."

Harry Dewitt was her boyfriend, twenty-seven years old, a revolutionary from San Francisco, thrown out even from Berkeley because of his penchant for mindless violence. She wondered, always, how she could divert that tendency into more rewarding channels. He was in Washington now, ferreting out secrets for Kirby. He had shaved off his beard, cut his hair, and taken to wearing a suit. A much wanted fugitive, he was passing himself off as a P.R. man with Mobil Oil, trying to insinuate himself into the good graces of anyone at a higher level who might just talk too freely.

Carolyne straightened up and Kirby said abruptly, "Show me your purse." She stared at him, but he repeated, "The purse."

Coldly, she handed it to him, and he shook the contents onto the bed. He found Harry Dewitt's photograph, looked at it for a moment, and then tore it into small pieces, tossing them to the floor. He said: "Nearly two hours, baby. Get your clothes off."

She hesitated. He sat up suddenly and reached out to her, taking hold of her wrist and pulling her brutally down on the bed, beside him. "If I take them off for you, they're all gonna get torn." He was already pulling at her shirt buttons, exposing the white skin of her breasts, mauling them, trying to get her belt undone. He sank his teeth into her and ripped at the shirt, and she said angrily, "For Chrissake..."

He held her down easily and laughed. "I'm going to have it, baby, one way or the other. You think you're going to stop me?"

He began tugging at the shirt again, and she said, "Wait, that's the only shirt I've got with me."

He let her go, then, lying back and watching her undress. *Well, not fat, really. Just too much of her here and there, but not bad, not bad at all.*

She dropped the shirt to the floor, took off the ceramic pendant and laid it on the table, pulled her jeans and panties off and stood there naked and angry, looking down at him with almost a snarl on her face.

"You're not going to like it very much, I promise you that," she said.

"Better than sitting on my butt for the rest of the day,

baby. Get on your back and open your goddam legs."

She lay down beside him without moving and let him take her, roughly and inconsiderately, without emotion of any kind. When Descartes came at two minutes before six, they had locked up the suitcases, Carolyne had placed the timers in the closet under the spare blankets, and they were ready to leave.

It was part of Kirby's policy—never more than four hours in the same place. At one time the maximum had been one day, but the cops had broken in on them once, and there had been a shootout. Carolyne had killed the officer who was holding a gun on Kirby—a single shot through the neck with a Colt 45. Now the limit had been cut to four hours.

Four hours here, then move on to another four hours there, and another four somewhere else, never any longer except in the safety of the swamp, where the redoubts were not only impregnable but so skillfully hidden that no one would ever find them.

The swamp was their sanctuary. Outside it, in a world that was as hostile to them as they were to it, the succession of grubby, squalid meeting-places was just part of the discomfort they all had to endure.

Descartes was driving a stolen car, and Carolyne told him about Strickland's wife. He nodded briefly.

Twenty-eight miles down the road, heading west on Highway 41, they stopped and took out the transmitter. There was desolate marshland all around them, an immensity of it, the telephone wires running on forever. A solitary chopper was cruising, far away to their right.

Kinono was standing by, waiting for the signal, and Carolyne said briefly, "Six AM., Point Baker, confirm."

Kinono's voice had a strange, melodic lilt to it, even over the static. "Point Four at six in the morning, confirmed."

She put the box under the seat and swung round to look at Simon Kirby. She thought that he was fast asleep; but as she stared at him, not liking him very much but knowing he was the best leader they could ever hope to find, the man who had brought them all together, he opened his one eye and stared back at her.

His haggard, gaunt, and deeply lined face, burned to the color of leather by the elements, was quite without any feeling on it.

He said, not even grinning at her, "We're going to do that again sometime, baby. Sometime soon."

She did not answer him. She swung around again, settled down in the seat, and watched the endless road in silence.

CHAPTER 5

Atlantic Ocean.

Coordinates: 80.01E
               26.02N

Everybody on board hated the plane. But it was one of Colonel Tobin's favorite toys, and the passengers were reluctantly learning to put up with its intense discomfort.

It was the intensively modified Dassault Mirage III-R, on which the Colonel had spent close to half a million dollars in modifications alone. It was unarmed; both Defa 5-52 cannon had been removed, as well as the huge bulk of the Omera Type 31 cameras.

Now the five men lay immobile in the niches that had been made for them, flat on their backs with no room even to scratch. Cass Fragonard, the gruff old Frenchman (a Sergeant in the Private Army now), eased himself around and tried to get his flask of good French cognac to his lips. The third of the delicate mid-Atlantic refueling operations was over, and the plane had roared up once more to its maximum speed, Mach 1.2 or 925 miles per hour.

It was low over the water, skimming the waves, and Drima, the Maltese navigator, said plaintively, "Take her up a bit, you bloody Italian. I'm getting my feet wet just looking at it."

Moretti, the young pilot, laughed. He dipped the nose a trifle and said, "Anyone want to fish?"

Curled up in the forward fuselage bay that had once held ammunition for the cannon, Major Paul Tobin, the Colonel's son, was gently trying to ease Drima's foot out of his face. He squirmed around to look at the illuminated hands of his watch and spoke into the intercom at his throat, "Ten more minutes, and we'll be climbing. Everybody stand by for trouble, ten minutes from now."

Trouble...It had to be expected. The coastal radar here was good, and at all but the very highest echelon, this was a top-secret operation. It had to be that way.

The Colonel had said defiantly, "No, Mr. Wagnall. I will not accept help of any kind, because in my book that...spells a loss of the absolute control I must have. And that includes my transportation. I have the necessary facilities, and I dare say they're a deal more practical than yours."

Wagnall had said mildly, an elegant eyebrow raised, "You surely don't expect to *smuggle* a small army into the United States; do you, Colonel?"

"Yes, sir, I do."

"Our coastal defenses are really quite efficient. I'd hate to see your men shot out of the sky by our fighters. Or their ship sunk by the Coast Guard."

"You're probing, Mr. Wagnall. I won't have it."

"Colonel, there's not a hope in hell you'd ever get away with it. At least let me get your men over the border."

"No sir. I will let you know, perhaps, when we are ready to go into action, and certainly when that action is over. In the meantime; just assume that as from the eighth of the coming month, the affairs of the Committee for Anti-American Activities will begin to wither. And that shortly thereafter, they will cease altogether."

"The eighth?"

"Yes. And by the fourth, I want all your operations against them whatever form they may be taking, to be suspended absolutely. Completely, and absolutely."

Wagnall had sighed. It was their second meeting in the lovely old London house; he had been summoned there most peremptorily. But then, the glorious Pamela Charles had been watching over him like a solicitous, gentle mistress, filling his glass with the Colonel's best Irish whiskey the moment he put it down empty.

At last, in the face of her charm and the Colonel's own stubbornness, he had given way.

And now, it was the ninth of the month. The advance contingent was moving into place.

There was Paul Tobin himself, the best goddamn soldier since Alexander, slim, fit, deeply tanned, his hair tousled above his freckled face, his pale blue eyes sharp and alert. There was Major Bramble, a great, hulking bear of a man in his late forties whose hobbies were hard drinking and the plump little body of Betty de Haas. There was Efrem Collas the Israeli, expert on unarmed combat and a great linguist. There was the young Brazilian, Manuel, who knew every one of the forty-seven-thousand types of plants that grew in his native Amazon and could survive, un-accoutered and stark naked, where ordinary men would perish.

And there was Cass Fragonard, with his two legs of aluminum—his own legs lost in Algeria—but still one of the best fighting men in the Private Army, pushing sixty and tough as a thirty-year-old. Somehow, he had contrived to smuggle on board a long loaf of French bread, half a pound of butter, and a wedge of Brie that Pamela Charles had bought for him at Fortnum and Mason's. Now he was eating contentedly, lying on his back in the greatest possible discomfort and making himself a cheese sandwich to go with the cognac without which he would under no circumstances stir from his quarters in the Colonel's house. The cognac was his viaticum, his security blanket and his comfort. It reminded him of the beautiful vineyards in the France he could never forget, the France to which he could never return. Back home he had killed, with his bare hands, three Corsicans who had attacked his granddaughter. And one of the Corsicans had powerful friends in the wrong places.

Bramble said, "If I don't get another two inches of space on my next trip in this bloody plane, you're going to have to leave without me."

"Ten more minutes," Paul said, "and you'll have all the space you can use." He knew that Bram hated parachuting more than anything in the world.

Moretti said suddenly, "Radar locked onto us. They're getting smart down there. We're supposed to be underneath it."

"Time to target?" Paul's voice was urgent.

Drima spun the needle on his chart. "Four minutes to the first turn, coastline coming up now, eighteen degrees right."

He hated the sound that came from the scanner, the long, insistent whine of the radar check. He said, and his voice was anxious, "Paul, I've got to lose it. They may not want to argue with us too much."

"Do what you have to do, Moretti."

He felt the plane swing round in a sickening turn that pressed him tight into the bulwark, and he knew that Bramble would be going out of his mind back there. He felt its nose go down, and saw that it was skimming over the water at maximum speed, heading on the wrong compass-bearing, out to sea again, and he waited for a reprise of the sharp turn that would bring them back on course once more.

Moretti said cheerfully, "Don't worry, I won't do that again. The wings on this *disgraziata macchina* are going to fall off, and then where will we be?" In a moment, he said, his voice controlled now, "Okay, we've lost it. Heading back on alternate course. Try and keep your feet out of the water."

They felt the plane swing round again, more gently now; it seemed as though the fuselage were cutting a swathe over the whitecaps. Suddenly a searchlight hit them, brightly illuminating the aircraft's interior. Moretti swung up and round and did a roll out of it, throwing the heavy plane around like a balloon with the air let out. Bramble: said, "Good God, man, don't ever do that again..."

The beam was behind them, and the plane went incredibly lower, seeking airspace where there was none, racing over land now and brushing the treetops. "We've lost the radar," Moretti said. "We're on our own again, but they know we're here. We ought to expect some sort of action pretty soon now."

A moment later, Drima said, "Twelve degrees right, first man ready."

Paul said; "That's you, Bram, are you ready?"

"Ready." He was watching the green light flicking on and off just above his eyes. "I'll be glad to get out of this coffin, parachute or no parachute. How many feet have I got?"

"Right now, none at all," replied Moretti. In four minutes exactly, I'm taking you up to four hundred feet. That's all you're going to get. Isn't that nice?"

"Christ."

Paul said, "Colonel's orders, Bram."

"Jesus Christ, the ejector's going to bury me in the mud."

"It's an interesting thought. Feet first, planted for eternity, with all the little Brams bursting forth in the spring."

The plane swept sharply upward. Drima yelled "Now!" and hit the red button that set off the explosive charge. Bram felt himself hurtling out like a ball from a cannon, and it seemed to him that the darkness of the swamp was no more than ten feet below him. The black parachute opened and the plane was gone, diving again now and veering round to the left for the second drop.

Drima said, "Manuel, eighteen seconds, stand by. Cass, you still have ninety seconds, just time to stow your Cognac aboard so's you can leave it behind. I'm thirsty."

Cass Fragonard braced himself for the shock of ejection. He had never told anyone, but the speed of the exit always seemed to tear the steel cables out of his legs, and he winced, feeling the pain of it already.

"Number Two, Go!" Drima said, and hit the button again. Manuel was airborne, floating easily down to the swamp.

Three more to eject now. The plane swung round thirty-one more degrees and dropped to zero feet—and the activator showed that coastal radar had found them again.

Drima was peering at the illuminated dial, its pale blue color weird and ghostly, and he said mildly, "Fighter plane moving in on us, eight miles distant, dead behind us; he'll catch up when we slow for the drop."

"How long have we got?" Paul asked.

"Two minutes fifteen."

"Get up high, then drop down fast."

"Roger."

Moretti shoved the throttles forward and stood the plane on its tail. Exactly one minute and forty-five seconds later he dropped it down again in a steep incline, racing down to treetop level and skimming low, and the Atar 9C3 turbojet, rated more than thirteen thousand pounds s.t. with after-burning, cut back sharply for the dangerous braking operation. Paul could feel his stomach driving itself up into his head.

Moretti hit the explosive capsule button again, and Number Three was in the air, Cass Fragonard with his sandwich still clutched in his hand, the cognac flask firmly buttoned into his inside pocket.

"The fighter?" Paul asked.

"Behind us, three miles, two thousand feet."

"Seed your foil."

"Roger." Moretti released the millions of strips of tinfoil that would throw off the pursuer's radar, at least for a while.

Efrem Collas, next to go, said suddenly; "I forgot to say goodbye to my girl," and Paul laughingly replied, "Send her a postcard, you stupid bastard."

The braking again, and it seemed as though the plane was standing still, tearing its guts out with the shock of deceleration, and again, Paul felt his insides turning over. Four of the lights on the control board were blinking steadily blue now, four of the men out and one to go:

He said, "All right, Moretti, get this beautiful toy home safely, you have the refueling points?"

"Yes, sir."

"You'll be back in London in time for breakfast. Have a couple of kippers for me."

Moretti said, "*Mannaggia!* The terrible things the British eat for breakfast!"

"Don't let that fighter shoot you down."

"No, sir. Ten seconds."

He watched the light, and when it turned to red he felt the shock of the propellant hit him, and then the twenty-eight-foot parachute was black above him in the black sky, and the plane was gone, streaking at maximum speed towards the coast and safety.

He switched on his R-phone as he floated down, and said, "Come in by numbers, you can talk in clear."

"Bram here—in position—no problems."

"Manuel here—okay."

"*Ici Cass. Tout va bien, movi vieux, sauf que*...lost my Brie sandwich up there somewhere."

"Efrem Collas, in position."

Paul hit the trees and switched off. In the damp night air, the drop was gentle, and he hung there, peering at the dark ground below him, unable to see how far down it was. He uncoiled the nylon rope from around his waist and slithered carefully down it, hand over hand till his feet were in deep mud.

He stored his gear and then climbed back up again, cutting the parachute clear and bringing it all down for burial in the dark and stinking morass. The frogs croaked their annoyance at him as he worked, and when he was finished, he pushed deeper under cover, found a dryish bank to sleep on, lay down in his aluminized sheet, and waited for the first streaks of dawn.

The advance contingent of Colonel Tobin's Private Army was in position.

Tomorrow, the hard work would begin. But for the rest of the night, there was only sleep. He took a long drink of Irish from his field service flask (solid silver, a present from the Colonel to each of his men) and closed his eyes.

And at five-thirty precisely, he switched on the miniaturized transistor sender that had been designed by Edgars Jefferson and his staff of expert technicians, and said, his voice very low, "Five-thirty. Rick, you should be there."

The voice in his ear seemed to come from close beside him. "I'm here, Paul. Are you on pinpoint?"

"Yes, I am—give or take half a mile or so. We had to take some evasive action back there. My God, the Colonel's right about that plane. The games Moretti plays with it...All the others are in position too; they should be starting to move on now."

"Then take a course of a hundred and seven for three and a half miles. There's a stream there, running northeast to southwest. Go southwest for eight hundred yards, where it forks. Take the right fork and go another three-quarters of a mile. That's where I'll be at eight o'clock. A houseboat. You'll be watched coming in, but don't worry about it—a Seminole Indian up in a tree and a couple of scary girls with shotguns. They're on our side, almost."

"But not quite?"

"Subject to confirmation. A good drop?"

"Perfect. How's Rena holding up?"

"She's fine. She's still asleep beside me, wedged in under the roots of a mangrove tree as big as a ten story house. She's lost a bit of weight on this trip, and she didn't start out with too much, did she?"

Paul could heat her indignant voice, picked up by the ultra-powerful mike: "I'm wide awake, and there's nothing wrong with the shape of my body."

He grinned: "Say hello to her from me. See you both at eight o'clock."

He shouldered his heavy pack and set off on a course of a hundred and seven degrees. The others, he knew, would by now be beginning their huge individual circles, searching, probing, exploring, the preliminary tactic the Colonel had insisted upon. "Know your ground," he had said. "Know exactly where you are and what's around you. It's virgin territory for all of you. And soon it'll be your battleground."

He sloughed his way along through the mud and the black waters of the swamp.

CHAPTER 6

Coral Gables.

Coordinates: 80.04E
                 25.92N

They were both senior members of the CAAA; Group Leaders, Kirby called them.

There was Suleiman Descartes, the Algerian who was part French; and Bjelovaci, the Serb. Descartes was twenty-one years old, an intense, nervous youth who wore, always, heavy leather bands around both his wrists and a thin steel chain around his neck. The chain was for strangling. Before he had been brought into the Organization through a breakaway segment of the Panthers, he had been merely a professional killer, hiring himself out to anyone who would pay his small price, because killing was a release for his constant anger. He was small and dark, a touch of black blood from the Fezzan in him somewhere. His mother had been a prostitute in the Algerian Casbah, and he had never known his father, whom he believed to be a trader from Timbuktu. He was dressed now in a dark gray suit, a little shabby, with a white shirt and a black tie, and black, rubber-soled Hush Puppy shoes.

Bjelovaci was much older, nearly thirty, and had been a leader in the anti-Croatian movement in his home country until he had learned that the Americans, maintaining their ties with Tito, were secretly supporting the Croats by sending them, via West Germany and Turkey, very considerable supplies of illicit arms. And then, his sectarian hatred of all things Croatian, nurtured through centuries of internecine fighting and vendetta, had centered firmly on the Americans in general, and the CIA—which he was convinced was the guiding power of his enemies—in particular. When Kirby's scout had first approached him, he had listened carefully, with that peculiarly restrained Serbian intensity, and had thought about it, and had said at last, "Only if I can kill Americans, personally." The young scout, whose name was Harry Dewitt, had nodded. "That's the whole idea, man. Me, I'm. American too, but don't ever remind me of it, or I'll kill you myself, big as you are."

He was a barrel-chested man with strong, heavy shoulders and thick legs, with a bull neck for which he could never find a shirt large enough. He carried his long Serbian knife thrust up the left sleeve of his brown sports coat, and he walked with a pronounced limp, a shattered kneecap from one of his village encounters; it never seemed to worry him anymore.

They were cruising past the house now, along the tree-lined street with its neat, suburban gardens and heavily laden citrus trees, driving the new Dodge van that had been stolen earlier that morning. "It might be chased," Kirby had said, "and we don't want one of our own trucks pumped full of bullet holes..."

He pointed, flickering the ash of his cigarette. "There, the white picket fence..." There was a station wagon parked in the carport, a child's three-wheeled bicycle on the front lawn.

They pulled in to the curb and got out of the van. Leaving the motor idling and the rear doors open, they went boldly up to the front door and pushed the bell. There was no traffic at all in the street.

The door opened, and Jane Strickland was there, a

pleasantly chubby woman in her early forties, with gold-rimmed glasses and carefully set blonde hair piled atop her head.

She was smiling affably, wondering who they were. They looked like encyclopedia salesmen, only where was the sample case? Before she had time to say good morning to them, the big man shoved her hard, a calloused hand on her chest, and sent her sprawling to the floor. They were both inside the house, slamming the door behind them. The small man, who had the fiercest eyes she had ever seen, was running quickly up the staircase. The other lugged her unceremoniously to her feet, twisting an arm behind her and putting a hand over her mouth to stifle her screams.

He held her there till the dark little man—was he an Arab? She thought of the Black September and Munich—came running down. The latter had evidently gone quickly from one room to the other, because when he returned to the hallway, he said very softly, "No one except the kid, about seven years old, in the john, I locked him in." She could hear the muted hammering at the door upstairs.

The big man said, also very gently, whispering into her ear, "If you want your son's throat cut, you scream, okay?"

Numbly, she nodded, and he pulled the long, slightly curved knife from under his jacket and showed it to her. He said, whispering still, "You see? I'll just cut his throat; you want to feel the edge?"

She was terrified. She shook her head, and he said, "You come with us, and you don't say a goddam word. If not..." He gestured with the knife again, and she nodded. Behind and beyond her fears, there was only one thought, *get these maniacs out of the house...*

He took her by the arm and held her while the little man opened the door, looked out into the street, and waited till a cyclist had ridden by. Then she allowed herself to be led down the flagstone path to the gate and into the back of the van. He pushed her down onto the floor, and the dark little Arab climbed in with her, not menacing her but just staring at her with those fanatical eyes. In a moment the van was heading fast out of town.

She sat on the wooden bench seat and wondered how long it would take Bobby to break out of the bathroom and call the neighbors—or his father.

Highway 41 was straight as an arrow, and within the hour they were turning north and heading into the swamp. The Arab had not once spoken; and she sat there, and shivered.

Cass Fragonard sank down in the black and stagnant water with only his head above the surface, and watched the canoe glide past him. The Spanish moss was gathered around his head and shoulders, and they could have passed within two feet of him and not seen him.

He waited till the canoe had gone and then eased himself up onto the bank, running fast on his two tin legs along the bank of the stream, looking back from time to time to make sure there were no others. When he came to a better point of vantage, he hid himself and watched. The canoe was gliding silently to the opposite bank, and the four men aboard—in a uniform of sorts, gray drill pants and shirts with gray berets—climbed ashore and headed toward the heavy cover of the trees.

One of the men, without a doubt, was Simon Kirby himself; the taut, angry face with its black eye-patch was too easily recognizable to permit any mistake. The others—he could not begin to guess who they might be. They were all armed with the Kalashnikov submachine guns, and they carried hand grenades at their belts as well.

And then, even before they entered the shelter of the trees—they just disappeared. The ground seemed to open up and swallow them. Cass took the slim binoculars from the waterproof pouch at his side and stared.

He said at last, "Tiens, tiens, well, well..."

It was less than a hundred yards away, but to the naked eye it was no more than a cluster of shrubs among a thousand other shrubs. Through the powerful glasses, now, he could see the cut ends of the branches that hid it, see even the footsteps in the black mud that led to the concealed opening, a dugout of sorts, roofed over with logs and completely encased by trailing, living vines.

He studied it long and hard. But when he heard a scream coming from the hideout, he eased back deeper under cover, took out the tiny sender, and switching it on to the emergency frequency, whispered, "Come in Paul or Rick, come in please."

The plug in his ear was clicking slightly, telling him that the emergency crystal was open at the other end, and then Paul's voice was there, clear and low, "Come in, Cass, what is it?" He sounded impatient.

Cass said, his voice a zephyr, "A hideout, coordinates 073-815 exactly. It's about forty feet long by the looks of it, extremely well camouflaged, on the edge of the stream. Simon Kirby just went in there with three other men. I just heard a woman scream in there."

"Hold on, Cass."

At the other end, Paul and Rick Meyers, with Rena Susac, were in their own camouflaged shelter, high in the heavy branches of a mangrove tree, a ten-by-twelve platform draped over with a plastic awning and swathed in moss and vines on all sides. The control console had been set up there, and Rena was crouched beside it, watching its faint green and blue and red and amber lights and keeping the sound down to minimum.

Paul looked at Rick Meyers. "Can we make a guess, or not?"

Rick nodded, his dark, intelligent eyes worried. "We can guess, but it's a long shot."

The report had come in four hours ago: Captain

71

ALAN CAILLOU

Strickland's wife had been kidnapped, the letters "CAAA" scratched on the plaster wall of the hallway with the point of a knife.

He said again, "A long shot, very long. But there's an alternative, isn't there?"

"One of *them* in trouble?" Paul was thinking of the girl who had been found, with her three companions, wire-strangled at the tree not more than a mile from this point.

"Could be. But as far as Cass is concerned, he has no option, has he? Whichever way it lies."

Paul took the mike again from Rena: "There's a good chance; Cass; it might be useful, one way or another; chances about eighty, I'd say. What's your estimation on getting in there and getting her out?"

Cass grinned to himself, a show-off. "One hundred, *mon Commandante*. There is a woman in there in trouble, and I will get her out with no problem at all. But that is not the question, is it? I have a chance to kill Simon Kirby now. It might save us all a lot of trouble. And the others there, I can kill them too. Maybe we cut down the odds a little, *n'est-ce pas?*"

Paul sighed. "It's tempting, but it's...one of those things, Cass. If we go off half-cocked, the Colonel will have my guts for a necktie; yours too. We're not ready; we can't go at this thing piecemeal, much as I'd like to take advantage...Play it by ear, Cass. Just remember that we really need their leader alive to keep them all together till we're ready to hit them. Play it by ear. Get that woman out and find out who she is. Come back on emergency when you're ready. Anything else?"

"*Oui, mon Commandante.* I've nearly finished my cognac, I'll have to pull out for supplies soon."

"Go to hell, Cass."

"*Oui, mon Commandante.*"

"And good luck."

Cass sniffed. "Luck? I am Cass Fragonard; I do not need

72

luck."

"Then out."

Cass tucked his sender into its pouch, took out the binoculars again, and studied the ground very carefully. He paid particular attention to the upper branches of the trees. When he was satisfied that he could move in safety, he wormed his way further along the bank, looking for a place where he could cross undisturbed. He found one at last, a point where the two banks almost met, a small weir heavily studded with large blocks of oolitic limestone and up-ended trees that had been long dead. He moved across carefully and made his way back, halfway to where he knew the shelter was.

Now, *now* was the time for caution to the utmost extent. He lay on his back and studied the treetops. Easing a little further on, he studied them again. At last he found what he was looking for, what he was certain had to be there.

Draped around one of the lower branches of a cypress tree, covered over with moss and sedge and ferns, a single sentry was posted. Cass eased away gently, searched for others, and found none. Now the scream came to him again, louder and longer. He winced but would not hurry, and he crawled back and watched the sentry for a while, moving gently to the best possible point for what he had to do.

When he was ready, he took out the powerful little slingshot and a quarter-inch steel ball-bearing, pulled back the rubber to its fullest extent, took long and careful aim, and let go.

He heard the sound of the ball clip once though the leaves and saw it strike squarely in the center of the man's forehead, saw the sudden spurt of blood as it entered the skull, saw the sentry collapse across his perch and hang there. And again he waited for any betraying sound. There was none.

He put the slingshot away and quickly assembled the Carlson automatic, rapid-fire machine pistol, slipping in the fifty-load magazine of plastic bullets inside their light weight sabots, which would strip off after leaving the muzzle.

The Carlson was an extraordinary gun. Still on the classified list at the NATO Arms Research Laboratory in Stockholm, it had been acquired by Colonel Tobin, who had already modified and improved it in his own weapons lab, Edgars Jefferson in charge.

Inside its fourteen-and-a-half-inch stock, which was made of the immensely durable plastic known as URY877, there were cunningly fitted two alternate barrels, four fifty-load clips of bullets, the alternate breach for the firing of its own special projectiles (the pencil bombs), and a barrel extender for long-range accuracy. It was light, enormously powerful, compact, easily portable, and would fire single shots or cycle at an incredible 1,400 rounds per minute, faster than the famous German MG42 from which its mechanism had been derived. Its maximum range, with the extension, was 4,500 yards, its accuracy was astonishing, and it was probably the best light machine gun ever developed. The sound of it was distinctive, a short, sharp *phutt* of an explosion.

He eased the catch from single to rapid three, and crawled carefully up to the shelter to examine it at length from all sides, creeping around it silently and looking for other exits.

He gently placed a sticky mass of plastic nitro against what seemed to be its door (under the camouflage, it appeared to be of cedar planking), pressed in a tiny time-detonator set to sixty seconds, and stood back, crouched and ready to barge in.

The explosive blew the door wide open, a gaping hole in a solid bank of earth and wood, and Cass yelled out one word at the top of his voice, "*Merde!*" He charged in, his gun ready, his finger along the trigger guard.

Kirby, he saw, was swinging round with alarm, and the others there, eight of them in all, were staring in shock at the intrusion. One of them swore and raised a gun. Cass shot him dead with three quick bullets, a short burst, hating the use of three rounds where one would do. But he had made his point, and he said quickly, "No one moves, not even you, Kirby."

The picture froze.

The Carlson gun was pointed straight at Kirby's gut, and Cass said again, "Nobody moves. I cut you in half if you move. Like this."

He raised the barrel of the gun, easing the catch over to rapid five, and pulled the trigger, as brief a moment of fire as he could manage. A burst, of fifteen polyarmorine high-impact bullets crashed into the wall above their heads, cutting a line from one wall to the other. Cass eased the catch back to single and said gently, "Impressive little gun, is it not?"

Kirby said sharply, "Nobody moves."

"Turn your backs, all of you, *vite*."

Kirby said, "Everybody turns around." He knew that his life, the life of everyone there, was not to be taken now and he was waiting his chance. He said calmly, "You could easily kill us all if you wanted to."

"*Tiens, tiens*...If I have to, I will. Better you make no mistake."

Their backs were turned to him, and he let his eyes take in the roomy. Thirty feet long, with a padlocked door at one end of it (he was glad of the padlock, no one in the other, smaller room) with camp cots, all folded, neatly stacked in a pile. A wooden table and cupboard, a battery light, a rack holding some forty rifles, all Kalashnikov semiautomatics, a pile of some twenty-four cases of hand grenades, a row of Coleman camp stoves on a shelf, a dozen or so wooden chairs...

The woman was tied to one of them, a middle-aged, frightened woman in a blue dress, her hair piled high on her head but now in disorder. There were twin knife-cuts down the sides of her face, deep and savage and bleeding heavily; the blood was staining the front of her dress, and she had been crying. Her eyes were swollen and red, and she was still sobbing as he looked at her. He said gently, "Which one cut you?"

She shook her head, too frightened to answer, and he said, "No matter..."

He had moved away from the gaping hole he had broken through and had taken up a position in the corner, his back to the wall, his gun ready. He said, "You, at the end there, untie her."

The man turned and looked at him coldly, unafraid, and said; "Untie her yourself, you bastard." He was a kid, not much more than eighteen or nineteen years old. Cass put a single bullet through the soft part of his thigh and said again, "Untie her."

The boy yelled in fury and pain, and fell to the floor. Cass said, "Get up, you're not hurt. Untie her." He added cheerfully, "Maybe. I ought to kill two or three of you, just for the hell of it, just for what you did to her."

The kid stumbled to his feet, hobbled over, and untied the cords that bound her. Cass asked, not looking at her, "Are you going to be all right?" He threw her a quick glance and said to the boy, "Back to the wall, and keep facing the other way. Anyone turns around, I kill him."

The woman nodded, and Cass said, sympathetically, "A little plastic surgery will take care of your face. It's all over now. Can you swim?"

Her voice was hesitant. "Yes, a little..."

"The stream's not very deep, probably...Cross over to the other side, get into the bushes there, wait for me."

She nodded again. "I want...I want..." She was still shaking, and Cass said gently, "Not now, Madame. Go quickly. Wait for me across the stream, but keep out of sight. I'll find you."

She scuttled out the door. He waited and in the silence he said happily, "I don't suppose anyone has any good French cognac here? No, I thought not, *des vauriens*, a bunch of worthless bums, no quality at all..." His finger was on the catch, switching back to rapid one. He hated rapid-fire shooting, as the

Colonel did. One shot to kill one man, it was part of their philosophy; but here the odds were too great. The shock of the surprise was wearing off, and he knew that soon, someone would start something—probably Kirby.

Their backs were still turned. With one hand, he pressed a two minute detonator into a mass of plastic and tossed it carelessly in a corner. He counted the seconds and then began to move toward the opening, saying, "You'll have thirty seconds to get clear before this place goes up. Don't waste them trying to shoot me."

He counted, then turned and ran. A burst of gunfire followed him and he threw himself to the ground, rolling under cover and firing back. Then the shelter went up in a massive explosion, and he got up and ran, wondering how many of them had gotten out alive, or indeed if any one of them had been too slow. He rather thought they might move out of there fast and thought, *What a pity, I could have weakened, the opposition by just that much, their leader too...*

He raced across the weir, doubled back, and saw them— two of them, not Kirby—struggling through the water to get there ahead of him. He fired two rounds, killing them both, and then he was diving under cover and dragging her to her feet, hauling her along and running, whispering to her, "There is nothing to be afraid of, *ma petite*, just hold tight to me and keep quiet when I say keep quiet."

They slipped into deep cover and heard the shouting of the men who were searching for them. Then he made a wide, wide detour with her and kept her moving until he was sure she was safe.

He pulled out his silver flask and handed it to her. She shook her head and said, trembling, "No, no. I'm all right now, really I am. And I don't drink, either. I don't find it necessary."

He was shocked. He said firmly, "Even so...Drink. There are times in everyone's life, and this is the time in yours. Drink, there's only a little left, and this, for you, is an emergency. Tell me your name."

"Jane Strickland. My husband..."

"Ah yes, of course."

She took the flask now, sipped from it gingerly, and said, "It's good, it's...warming." She handed it back, looked at him, and said, her voice still shaky, "I really must thank you, Mr.—?"

"Cass Fragonard, *à votre service, chère Madame*."

"Mr. Fragonard...Did my husband send you? And how did you find me? When I saw that dreadful place, hidden away like that..."

Cass put a hand over his heart and said piously, "Saint Matthew said 'Seek, and ye shall find.' So I went seeking, and I found. He also said 'Knock, and it shall be opened unto you.' So I...knocked."

"You're a strange man, Mr.—What was it?"

"Fragonard. It means that I was born under a holly bush, but perhaps that's not quite true, I really do not know." He took his medical kit and applied a pad to each of the wounds on her face. "It will take a little time to heal, but these days...The doctors are very clever here. In a few months, it will not show at all." The cuts had gone down to the bone.

She began to speak, reaching out and touching him, and he said suddenly, "Sshhh..." When her eyes went wide with fright again, he smiled and put a finger to his lips and pointed. One of their searchers was struggling through the tangle of wet undergrowth, a hundred feet away and moving away from them. They waited a little while, and Cass said at last, whispering, "The danger is gone, but we must still be careful. I hold your hand, and we move very quietly. Come."

She looked around her. "In this terrible place...where can we go?"

"I will take you home. You speak French?"

She shook her head blankly, and he smiled: "No, I don't

78

suppose you do. You must excuse me."

He pulled out the little sender, threw the switch, and said in French, "*Le chef*, give me the chief."

Paul was there, speaking French too, but he said mildly, "State secrets, Cass?"

"No, *mon Commandante*, just sound common sense. The lady is the wife of the 'police officer, you know the one?"

"Ah good, good...Have you talked with her?"

"Not yet."

"Where are you?"

"Four miles from the road at 098.722. If you get a car there for her, I will have her there in two hours."

"Good. Is she all right?"

"*Ils l'ont coupé le visage un peu*, they cut her face up a little. She will recover."

"All right, get moving, 098.722, in two hours. Thanks, Cass. Out."

He put away the set and smiled at her, saving primly, "It is rude, they tell me, to carry on conversations in a language a guest does not understand. I ask your indulgence."

She was bewildered, and he helped her along. "Can you walk four miles in this, do you think?"

She nodded, and he said, "You will meet a man named Paul Tobin, He will want to know, what they hoped to find out from you. He is a friend, a good man. He'll take you back to your husband."

"They were trying to find out..." She was trembling again, and he held her hand tight and said, "A little more Cognac? It's a great healer."

She nodded, and he handed her the flask again, a little reluctantly. She sipped at it and said, frowning, "My husband, Captain Strickland, has been involved with a terrible thing called the CAAA, the Committee for Anti-American Activities, can you believe such a thing? But a few days ago, they pulled him off the

ALAN CAILLOU

case, just when he was beginning to get somewhere. You know how it is in government. They...they wanted to know *why*."

"And you told them? This way, through here, carefully..."

She crawled on her hands and knees after him through a tunnel of wet sedge, and said, "No, how could I? I didn't even know. The Captain was furious—well wouldn't you have been? Just when he was doing so well? Oh dear, I tore my stocking..."

She laughed suddenly, a short, unexpected laugh. He wondered if she was already a little high and took his beautiful silver flask away from her, shaking it sadly; it was empty now. She said, "It frightened me when you half blew the place up, scared the hell...oh dear, it scared the wits out of me, but I saw their faces. You should have seen them. The one with the patch on his eye is Simon Kirby, the head of the CAAA, and he was calling one of the others Bellamy, or a name like that, I think, or maybe Bellflower. Does that help?"

"It all helps." He let her talk, knowing it was therapy for her. At one point they heard the sound of firing, a long, long way behind them, and when she started he said,

"They are shooting at shadows, very angry men."

"Oh. Are you from the CIA?" Her voice was a whisper.

"The CIA? Oh no,"

"Ah. Then you must be FBI, such nice men always..."

The darkness of the swamp, somber and humid, was lightening now. The last of the Spanish moss was behind them, the wet sedge almost all gone. There were no more mangroves, only tall and gnarled cypress trees. When they reached the dirt road that led, eventually, to the highway, the car was there and Paul and Rena were waiting.

They helped Mrs. Strickland aboard, fussing over her solicitously. Paul, grinning, handed Cass Fragonard a new bottle of his favorite cognac, and said gruffly, "Get back into the swamp, Cass. You're beginning to look like an animal—go live like one."

Cass, tucking the bottle happily under his belt, asked, "How are we all doing, Paul? How many hideouts?"

"They're more than hideouts, Cass; they're strongpoints, redoubts. Manuel came up with three, Efrem another three, the Old Man and his daughters are getting more helpful by the hour. Plus yours..."

"I blew mine up."

"Six, then, already located. There have to be more. And we have to find them. Rick's working on it, it's not easy."

"*Bien sûr*. We need a break, a slice of that luck you offered me."

"We'll make our own. Get back, Cass, be on your way. Keep up the good work. Anything moves, anything at all, follow it and run it to ground."

Cass turned away. Mrs., Strickland was leaning at the window, reaching out. He went to her, and putting her hand on his arm, she said: "How can I ever thank you, Mr. Fragonard? *Monsooer Fragonard*?" He patted her hand and beamed at her.

The car drove off, and Cass watched it go. With a sigh, he turned his back on the hot sunlight and went back to the fetid stench of the swamp to continue his search.

CHAPTER 7

Frogleg Creek.

Coordinates: 81.06E
                26.12N

It was Rick Meyers who manufactured the good fortune.

It was always Rick Meyers. He was, without a doubt, the best Intelligence officer Colonel Tobin could have found anywhere, a shrewd persistent man with a darkly inquiring mind, devious to a point of Machiavellian cunning.

Sitting with Paul in their treetop H.Q. deep in the swamp, he had said, "Paul, what we've got, what we're getting...It's not going to be enough. Bramble wants to go in there and knock the hell out of them, but the trouble is...we don't really know enough of the background stuff, the background that makes for good tactics."

Paul waited. He wondered what Rick had up his sleeve.

Rick Meyers went on, "As always, the Colonel has refused any help, and as always, he's right. But from what we know of Strickland, he must have amassed a considerable amount of the kind of information I need. It's a shame; isn't it, that we don't have access to his files?"

"Go on."

Rick stood up and began prowling, gesticulating quietly,

his voice low and measured. "I want to put one of our people in with *them*, and that's not really too difficult. What's more of a problem, I want to get one of *them* to come over to us. And for that...I need to know a lot more than I know now."

Paul was still frowning about the first part of the suggestion. "Not easy to infiltrate them, either. Kirby's 'going to take a lot of convincing that someone's not being planted on him," he replied.

"Not if it's done the right way. Not if it's the right girl."

He was startled, "Girl?"

"Rena."

"My God..." He looked across at Rena, getting some food ready for them. The temptation to veto the idea at once was strong, but he said instead, "You've discussed it with her, of course?"

"Yes, I have."

"And she agrees?"

Rena said lightly, "Of course I agree. That's what field work is about and that's what I want."

"I don't like it."

"You forbid it?"

"No. But I want to be sure that maximum security is secure enough."

"It will be. And if I can get one of *them* on our side too, then we've got it made."

The crickets and the frogs were laboring, one against the other, filling the evening air with their discord. The gray mist was heavy on the swamp, reaching close up to the crow's nest, so that it seemed as though a delicate carpet of tangible mist was just below them; it was a temptation to step out onto it, to be borne away on its fragile, weaving surface.

The reports were coming in from time to time, with Rena at the console plotting the enemy hideouts on the chart, but away from it now because of the darkness, when everything stopped.

She was making them both sandwiches and filling the little shot glasses (no reason for discomfort, even here) with the Colonel's Irish—the Staff Irish, he called it.

The crude shelter was beginning to look like home. The wooden plank floor was covered with a heavy thickness of carpet, not for luxury but to silence their footfalls. The control console was set like a modernistic dresser to one side, its faint lights constantly glowing. There were four canvas chairs and a collapsible table, and three carefully shaded battery lights which cast a pale amber glow over the shelves that held their food supplies, the small glasses, and the three bottles of Irish. The sleeping bags were rolled up, doubling as comfortable seats, and one wall was hung with the large-scale charts of the Everglades, carefully annotated in Betty de Haas fine hand, with small-scale maps to one side with their relevant connotations in red, yellow, and blue ink. It looked like a campaign headquarters, with the added touch of luxury from the glassware that reflected the amber lights.

And outside, there was always that magic carpet of mist that seemed to leave them suspended in limbo, with only the dense, concealing shrubbery of the treetops to remind them of the swamp below.

Rick looked at his watch. "Seven-fifteen. I wonder if Strickland works late in his office?"

Paul shook his head. "Tonight? Almost certainly not, Rick. He just got his wife back, and he's not the man to stay late at the office while she's in the state she's in. But there's something else that's been bothering me. His reaction."

"Yes, me too. When he saw those knife-cuts on his wife's face...He's liable to have a hundred men out looking for the CAAA tomorrow, orders or no orders. Of course, it might not do too much harm; it might drive them toward the sort of consolidation that's best for us. But it might disperse them too, and we just can't have that."

"And we can't have his men getting in our hair, either. I think I'd better talk to the Colonel. Wagnall's the only man who can make sure that the interference stays where it is, at zero."

Rick was smiling faintly. "And perhaps we'd better not mention what we're planning to do."

"All right." He looked at Rena, spreading the *foie gras* carefully, making sure that everyone got a fair share of the truffles. "Get the Colonel for me, will you Rena? On scrambler, I want to talk in clear."

She put down the knife, and wiping her hands carefully, sat at the console, pushing buttons. The twin red lights showed that the conversation would be scrambled at source, unscrambled from jargon at the other end. In a few minutes, Pamela Charles' voice was there, low and controlled and feminine. Rena turned the sound down and said, "Pam? How's foggy London?"

"It's fine, Rena, you want the Colonel?"

"Paul wants him."

"Hold on, I'll get him. He's in the bath."

In a few moments, Colonel Tobin was there. Paul could visualize the big blue towel round his father's tight, muscular waist, the water dripping onto the expensive Axminster carpet. He said, "Paul? Good to hear from you. How are you? Scrambler's on this end, you can talk in clear."

"Yes, sir. We're on schedule, but only just. We believe that Strickland may possibly—almost certainly—be contemplating disobeying his orders and taking some action on his own."

"Oh? What makes you think that? I'll have his guts for garters if he does."

"They kidnapped his wife and beat her up..."

"The devil they did!" He could sense the shock at the other end. "His wife? Good God. You'll get her back, of course?"

"It's already been done, sir. Cass Fragonard got her out."

85

"Ah yes, Fragonard, a good man. Such a pity he's French; he'd have made a good Englishman. So?"

"Well, from my assessment of Captain Strickland, I'd say he's liable to go charging in there to settle the score himself. And apart from any other considerations, he's liable to find *us*—we're right in the middle of them. I thought you might have a word with Wagnall."

"I will indeed. It shouldn't be difficult. That letter, by the way."

"Ah, Wagnall's letter."

"It was from the President. Really quite charming—he has a nice command of diplomatic language. I'm glad Wagnall didn't have to produce it—makes me feel a little smug, and I enjoy that. When will you be ready for Main Force?"

"We're still plotting their hideouts. Bram's making up the charts. We still need more info, and Rick's planning on getting it." He looked across at Rick's face, dark and alert in the faint amber lights. "Tonight. We should be ready in three, four days, no more. Then it's a question of getting them where we want them."

"Have you decided how to do that?"

"No, sir. Not yet."

"My God, I think I'd better come over there and take charge myself then."

"A few more days, sir, we'll manage."

The Colonel's voice was suddenly very gentle. "Yes, Paul, I'm sure you will." He loved his son dearly and knew his talents. "No mosquitoes in that damned swamp?"

"Plenty of them."

"Then I hope you're taking your mepacrine tablets, all of you?"

"No, sir. The Irish is better."

"Ah, yes. How's Rena holding up?"

"Making us *foie gras* sandwiches at the moment. Holding

up fine."

"Good. Don't worry about Strickland; I'll have a word with Wagnall. Charles is already trying to reach him at his emergency number. Anything else?"

"That's all, sir. Everyone says to say hello."

"Then give them all my best wishes. I want this thing over soon, Paul. I want you all home again. Out."

The line went dead, and Rena flicked the switches and went back to her household chores. Paul said quietly, "It'll take you three hours to get to Strickland's place, Rick. You'd better be on your way. Make sure no one gets hurt."

Silently, Rick Meyers dropped the long rope down from the shelter. He stuffed a sandwich into his pocket, took a long drink of medicinal whiskey to keep the mosquitoes at bay, and slid down into the gray mist.

The office was easier than he could ever have imagined.

It was on the seventh floor of the Universal Bank Building, discreetly described on the board as the "Office of Mutual Care and Assistance," and he was grateful that Strickland, demanding complete secrecy for his operations, had insisted on keeping out of the well-guarded federal building.

Easy enough to break in anywhere, he was thinking, but if no one has to get hurt...

He went up in the elevator, picked the burglar-proof lock in twelve seconds, and let himself in, using his pencil flashlight to explore the offices. He found the tiny electric eyes, bypassed them all, put the burglar alarm out of commission expertly, and picked the locks on all the filing cabinets till he came to the right one.

It took him nearly half an hour to find all the files he wanted. When he was through, he scrawled the letters "CAAA" on the top of Strickland's beautiful walnut desk, let himself out, locked the door behind him, and went on his way.

By two-fifteen in the morning, he was back at the treetop H.Q., whistling softly for the long rope to be lowered to him. He sent up the heavy bundle of files first, then swarmed lightly up after them.

Rena was awake and waiting for him, with hot coffee, a neat little pile of *foie gras* sandwiches in Saran Wrap, and a glass of the Staff Irish to warm his bones.

He kissed her quickly on the cheek; patted her smooth behind, and sat down with Paul Tobin to study the first of the files. It seemed that Strickland, a thorough and probing man, had gathered an immense amount of information, and Rick said, gloating, "This is exactly the kind of thing I need. Exactly."

He speed-read the pages, passing them over to Paul with occasional comments, his mind furiously at work.

By four-forty-five, he put the files down, leaned back in his chair, hands clasped behind his head, and stared up at the awning over the shelter for a while. He said at last, very sure of himself, "Carolyne Southby, Paul. She's the one I want. She's their weak link, and the one who can help us."

Paul nodded. "Yes, I think you're right. If we can swing it. But how, Rick? How?"

"Let me think about that for a while. There's the glimmer of an idea at the back of my mind."

"The most devious mind in history."

"I'll have an answer for you in the morning. The more I think of it, the more I like it. Yes, Carolyne Southby."

Rena had sorted the pages from the files into their separate packages, the trivia on one side, the more important on another, and the really important intelligence neatly bound in a red folder. At five o'clock in the morning, they climbed into their sleeping bags and closed their eyes.

At five-thirty, Rick said softly, "I've got it, Paul. If she's really in love with Harry Dewitt, her boyfriend...Yes, she's as good as ours already. See you in the morning, Paul. Goodnight."

The morning? In half an hour it would be almost daylight. He reached out and groped for Rena's body, touching it. Her hand was there, waiting for him, and he held it tightly and fell asleep.

Captain Strickland had decided to stay home for the morning. The young doctor had come, looked at the scars, and had recommended the plastic surgeon. Strickland had declared, "Honey, there's no power in the world going to drag me down to the office today..." He was still fuming at the orders he had long ago received, and he was on the verge of saying, *the hell with them*. But they had come, he had been told, from the White House itself; it was a mystery that puzzled and disturbed him.

He knew something was afoot; but the answer to the question eluded him—*what?*

It was six-thirty in the morning. He was making the coffee and trying to cope with the batter for the waffles. His wife, her shock not gone yet, was still in bed.

The phone rang. "Strickland here, and I don't want to be disturbed today..." He broke off, the red suffusing his face again, and ran upstairs to his wife. "Those sonsabitches!" His voice rose in anger. "They broke into my office during the night and stole all my secret files. I'm sorry, honey, I've got to go in. I can't help it." She was staring at him, frightened by the memory. "Those terrible people..."

"Now don't you fret, honey. Joey and Bill are outside the house. They're going to take good care of you."

He was back in his own room before she could speak, and in a few moments she heard him run down the stairs and slam the front door shut. She heard him yell to the guards who were now there, a phrase she could not catch but which sounded like "You take good care of Mrs. Strickland, now..." and then, smelling the burning waffle batter, she went downstairs to turn out the gas and start over.

She heard the car start up and screech out of the garage, the siren blaring its fury, and she began to cry quietly.

Strickland's rage was savage. He found the scrawled letters on his desk, bawled out the guard who had found them there, and ordered the locks to be changed, wondering how they'd gotten hold of the keys (he did not believe the locks could be picked, the Department had assured him of that), and wondered also, fretting about it, why the carbine hanging in its holster on the wall had not been stolen as well. He thought about the Pentagon Papers for a while, and wondered if there were anything in his files that might be embarrassing if made public, all the while staring at the carbine and not too happy at seeing it there.

He made up his mind, and said at last to his aide, "Jerry, you get that carbine over to H.Q. My guess is it's been tampered with. Have them take a look at the firing pin, look for maybe even a booby trap. They must think I'm an idiot if they think they can get away with that."

He took it down gingerly from the wall, inspected it briefly, and handed it to Jerry Rossiter, a good-looking young cop in his late twenties, and said again, "Just have them take a look at it for me."

He picked up the phone and dialed a number. He called Arthur Reddies, his number-two man, and said, very quiet and calm now, "Art? Get your arse out of bed and get on over here. We've got work to do."

He listened awhile to the complaints, then said, "They attacked Jane yesterday, and last night they broke into my office and took away all my confidential files. You think I'm going to sit still for that kind of crap? What I want you to do, Art, is round up some of the boys, say forty of fifty of them, we're going into...How's that? The hell with the Directive, I'm going in after them, you better believe it..." He sounded aggrieved. He said, "That's right, Art, you and me and forty, fifty of the men, we're going right into that swamp and we're going to find those sonsabitches. I don't care if it takes forever, we don't come out till we have a showdown with them...What? Well, we'll look until we find them. You just get your arse over here fast, meet me on the street down below..."

He slammed down the receiver, stared glumly at the wall for a moment, got to his feet, and strode out. He wished he'd stopped for some coffee, but now...Now, there just wasn't time.

He pushed the elevator button, decided not to wait for it, and ran down the seven flights, light on his feet for such a big man, and stood out in the early morning Florida sunlight, lighting a cigar and waiting for Arthur Reddies.

He stood firm on his broad feet, a thick-chested, slightly plump figure of a man with a scowl on his closely shaved, handsome face, his hair cropped fairly short, his uniform neat and well pressed. His hair was graying now, and the lines on his face were deep, the lines of long and conscientious service.

He was not a man to fool around with, Captain Strickland. Once he had found two of his men on the take, shaking down the nightclubs. He had called them into his office and pummeled the hell out of both of them, the best discipline he knew how to impose, beating them up and warding their fury away till they were bruised and bleeding and ready to listen to decent sense and then, no more about it because it was all over and forgotten. His older boy, Charlie, had died of leukemia at the age of thirteen, and ever, since then, he had lived for nothing more than his work and his wife, a good, devoted father and husband, and a fine cop—if a little too tough for his own good.

He watched the patrols going into the station house across the street, looked at his watch impatiently, and wondered where Arthur Reddies was...A slight, easy-mannered man was suddenly beside him, saying politely, "Chief Strickland? My name's

Wilbur Hanning, I'm from the Pentagon."

Strickland turned. Hanning was holding a card up for him to see. He took it, examined it carefully, handed it back, and said, "Well, Mr. Hanning? What can I do for you. I'm right busy just now, but if it doesn't take too long..."

Hanning said, smiling, "Not as busy as you would like to be, I'm afraid." He slipped a hand into his breast pocket and pulled out a letter, saying, "A reminder of certain directives you were given a short while ago. You recognize the signature, I presume?"

Strickland read the letter in stolid silence. When he had finished, he said, "Arthur J. Wagnall, yes I recognize it." He looked at the date of the letter—today's date, and it was only seven in the morning. "When was this letter written, Mr. Hanning?"

A thin, easy smile, "Shortly after midnight. It's genuine."

"Yes, I know that. That guy likes to stay one jump ahead of me, doesn't he? He must be some kind of mind reader."

"His deductions are perfectly correct. Perhaps that's another way of making the same statement."

"Six hours before I decide to do something, he writes me a letter saying don't do it."

"Yes. It's interesting, isn't it? Perhaps that's the faculty that has put him where he is, Chief Strickland."

"Just tell me how he managed to do that. To satisfy my own curiosity."

"I'd prefer not to discuss it, if you don't mind. I'm merely Here to see that your orders are carried out. If necessary, I have sufficient authority to have you arrested, but I'm sure it won't come to that, will it?"

The accent was Bostonian. Strickland was thinking, *the sonsabitches, all of them*. He said coldly, "No, it won't come to that." He grinned suddenly, his face lighting up. "But once they get my resignation, that authority would begin to dissipate, wouldn't it?"

"Your resignation?" Hanning asked gently. "Why don't you think about that for a while, talk it over with Mrs. Strickland for a few days. Just a few days, Chief, that's all."

"Oh? And what's going to happen in just a few days, Mr. Hanning?"

"I think you might find that in a few days, strictly between the two of us, things just might start returning to normal again."

"You mean that I can start chasing after those bastards again? Is that what you're trying to tell me?"

"I'm not trying to tell you anything. But the assessment at the White House is that...After a few more days, you may not have to."

He was quiet and persuasive and smiling. Strickland looked at him suspiciously and growled, "I wish I knew what the hell was going on around here."

Arthur Reddies pulled over in his patrol car, leaned out the window, and looked at them. "It's off, Art." Strickland said. "Just forget I called you. Get your arse back to bed again."

The smile had not left Hanning's face, a smile of quiet amusement. He said, "Good day, Chief it was nice meeting you."

He sounded as though he meant it. When he turned and moved off, Strickland noticed the two plainclothesmen who moved in unobtrusively behind him.

He grunted. He called for his car and went home to finish his breakfast.

CHAPTER 8

Frogleg Creek.

Coordinates: 81:06E
           26.12N

The files had shown one extraordinary thing: Strickland knew a lot more about the CAAA than he was given credit for.

There were forty-two pages on Carolyne Southby alone, and no less than a hundred and four on Simon Kirby. Harry Dewitt rated eleven, and there were twenty-three on the Japanese contingent, which had arrived in twos and threes via Cuba or Mexico over the past six months, smuggling themselves in with astounding ease.

Each of the Chief's previous efforts to capture the gang had resulted from his absolute certainty that, at the time of his operation, he knew exactly where they were. But the enormous difficulties of any paramilitary engagement in swamp territory, known so well to the enemy, had simply been too much for him.

Major Bramble, at present coordinator and the field officer responsible for planning, had joined Rick Meyers in the H.Q. crow's nest, and they were collating the various reports that had come in from Manuel, Efrem Collas, and Cass Fragonard. The master chart was now thickly covered with the pins that identified the strongpoints of the CAAA so far discovered. The aerial surveys, some of them from the photo-satellites, had been interpreted by Betty de Haas. Even she, the most skilled of all cartographers, had been able to find very little; the dense canopy of the swamp's foliage was too concealing.

But here and there, a break in the trees, or the course of a stream, or an opening in the canopy—these things had a lot to tell her. Day and night she had pored over the photographs and the charts of what she liked to call the "bounce-back radar," one of her favorite tools, checking the almost incomprehensible pinpoints and shadows and highlights.

A picture was emerging, but it was not clear enough. Ground surveillance, as the Colonel had shrewdly guessed from the very start, was the only answer. It was to be a long, patient, and dangerous operation. Paul's order had gone out, "You see a footprint, follow it. A canoe, follow it. Anything moves at all, follow it..."

Bramble was poring over the maps, marking the routes that could feasibly provide some sort of access and a reasonable campaign trail. He was sweating heavily, a red-faced, bluff sort of man from a past era, a professional soldier of the old school from Sandhurst in England and St. Cyr in France. His hearty, blustering manner masked a shrewd and determined mind, but not very well. He was the precise antithesis of Rick Meyers, and the two were close friends, poles apart in their philosophies but united by a fierce devotion to Colonel Tobin and to the work he was engaged in.

He picked up the red-bound file, studied it, and said, puzzling it out slowly, "Wouldn't you say that Strickland could have picked up Carolyne Southby any time he wanted to? Dammit, she has post office box in Miami, and so does Harry Dewitt. So why didn't he? They're both on the FBI's most wanted list."

To Rick, it was all perfectly clear; more, it made good sense. He said patiently, "Strickland had the same idea that we have. He didn't want to arrest one or two of their leaders, because they would have been quickly replaced. He wanted somehow, to get them all together. Or, when he thought they might be, his plan was to go in there after them. Only he never had *enough* information. His Intelligence is good, but not good enough. He always failed because he always went off half-cocked; it's a common enough mistake."

Bramble grunted. He was always restless under Rick Meyers' patient search for more, and always more, of the background information that was so necessary a part of his planning. He said, grumbling, "I believe Cass should have got Kirby while he had the chance the other day."

"No," Rick was very sure of himself. "Paul was absolutely right. Kirby can be replaced too. Sure, he's the organizational brain, but there are plenty of others too. The body doesn't always die—at least, not fast enough—when you cut off the head. You need to lop a few limbs as well. Besides, the Colonel would have had a fit. Half-cocked—Strickland's error."

Bramble nodded. "Well, perhaps you're right. I never like to argue with the Colonel's reasoning; it's usually right. When do you pick up the girl?"

Rick passed across a telegram. He said, frowning, "A higher degree of risk than I usually care to take, but I'm assuming that Harry Dewitt is out of contact with his girl. Not quite the longshot it seems, because it's obvious from Strickland's assessment that Kirby has his eye on Carolyne Southby himself."

He sighed. "I don't usually like to use other people's Intelligence; half the time it's not very good. But I've a feeling that Strickland is right. I believe that one of the reasons Kirby sent Dewitt to Washington was that it would give him an opportunity to get his hands on her. The personal side of a very impersonal man—it's often the lever by which he can be toppled. Therefore, I'll take Strickland's deductions as probably correct, and that's all Intelligence consists of, probabilities that turn out, in the course of time, to be certainties. Fair reasoning?"

"No," Bramble said. "But go on."

"Yes, there's an element of risk. That's the reason for the wording."

The telegram read, *Meet me Old Man's place urgentest secretest immediate. Bad trouble. Harry.*

Rick said, "*Secretest.* That means she won't dare check even if she is in contact with him. And the rest—it's a little bit gruesome."

"Gruesome?"

"The last thing Strickland did..." Rick sighed. He felt uncomfortable about what he had done, but knew it was necessary. "Strickland discovered four bodies in the swamp on his last sweep. They'd been strangled—you heard about it. The bodies were given a decent burial, you recall. Well, I had them dug up again."

"My God."

"A few men who weren't averse to earning a considerable amount of the Colonel's cash laid out the bodies for me to look at, in the dead of night in a dark, dark cemetery. It was not very pleasant. One of the men could easily be Harry Dewitt."

Bramble was staring at him, horrified, and Rick went on: "They'd been strangled, remember, and left there for some days. They were all bloated, half-eaten away by the insects, no hope of recognizing any one of them. I selected the one that was closest to Harry Dewitt's size and physical properties, and had it brought back into the swamp. Not too far away from here, as a matter of fact," he added mildly.

"My God..."

"Yes, it's not nice. It's been reburied, in the swamp, and the stage is set. And the rest is up to Paul. As I said, not very nice."

Bramble shuddered. He said grimly, "That's very true.

97

What's more, I'll make a small bet it's not going to work. Oh yes, I know what's in your mind. You're a devil, Rick Meyers."

"But a very capable one. I won't take your bet. You'd lose too easily—it wouldn't be fair."

"And if Harry Dewitt turns up unexpectedly?"

"He won't. I've pulled Efrem Collas out of the swamp and sent him to Washington to keep an eye on Dewitt. With the help of Strickland's dossier on him, it wasn't too hard to track him down. If he shows any signs of returning too soon...Efrem takes care of him."

Paul Tobin had installed himself in the old man's houseboat. He rather enjoyed the company there.

Old Man was drunk, so drunk he could hardly stand up. There were ten bottles of the Colonel's best Irish whiskey tucked away under one of the beds, another bottle, empty, on the floor in a corner, and another one, half-full now, clutched in his skeletal hand. And he was happy.

He said "I guess I ain't never bin so happy before, not since the last time I screwed the wife o' that Spanish General, what was his name now?"

Paul said, smiling; "Galvez."

"Yes, Galvez...That was way down in New Orleans. Them Spaniards had just declared war against England. Hell, I remember the date like it was only yesterday, 1779. I guess I wasn't more'n twenty, twenty-one years old then, a real red-blooded boy, I kin tell you. They got them a gunboat on the river, just a mite away from here, and fifteen-hundred Spaniards marched into the swamps, along the shoreline. There was a hurricane blowing, I recall, and they'd come from the British Forts on the Mississippi...Hell, them Spaniards had taken Fort Bute on Bayou Manchac; they'd captured Fort Panmure and Baton Rouge, and he was aiming to take Pensacola too, though maybe that was about a year later..."

His voice was slurred, but he was grinning cheerfully. He said, reminiscing, "I was just a boy then, and I recall that Galvez good. He brought in two thousand militia, black men, most of them, from...from...where was it now?"

Paul said, "From Havana, Old Man. He took Charlotte on Mobile River with them. In the year 1780."

"Yes, Havana...And Pensacola surrendered to him, didn't it? He took over the whole of West Florida, but when he set foot in these swamps...You know why he never as much as caught himself a gator here? Because I was leading the British out of the Everglades, and ever since then, that Galvez has bin after my blood, chasing me all over."

He broke off, frowning, and looked at the whiskey bottle. "Was that me, or was that my pappy? Hell I don't know for sure, mighta bin my grandpappy for all I know." He sighed, "No, it was me, I guess. A long time ago..."

Paul let him ramble on, enjoying the enjoyment itself, knowing the old man was completely mad, and glad to be still alive.

Beside him, the young Sarah lay on the bed, on her side, staring at him and sometimes reaching out to touch his leg, running the tips of her fingers along it idly. She eased herself closer to him and said, "You like me, Paul? You really like me?"

He put a hand at her waist and patted her gently. "Yes, I do, Sarah."

"You got a girl of your own? Back home, maybe?"

He shook his head and she smiled. "That's real nice."

She eased over closer and put her head in his lap, resting it on his thigh, one slim hand held under it, the fingertips still scratching lightly. Her rumpled dress was carelessly open, all over, her breasts firm and plump, her thighs enticing. She slewed around suddenly and looked up at him, her eyes wide and innocent. "You want to love me now? You want?"

He looked quickly at the old man, and Sarah said carelessly; "Oh, he don't mind none, he's used to it. Even with Flagstaff, he don't mind none."

He did not feel as restrained with her as his upbringing might have demanded; even her age did not trouble him, any more than it troubled her, and he was thinking again of the time when Man himself came out of the swamps, half fish, half animal, propagating his species on and now...Did they, too, feel the urges that were on him?

Her fingers were caressing, and he laid a gentle hand on her breast. He said, "Where is Flagstaff now?"

She shrugged. "He don't matter none."

"Where is he?"

"Oh, out in the swamp some place. Up in one o' them trees, I guess, like he always is."

"Maybe I'd better go and check with him."

He stood up and moved to the entrance, and Sarah sat up quickly and called after him, "You come back soon, now. I'm waitin' for you..."

He walked over the narrow plank to the share, looked around, and found the Seminole at last, well hidden in the upper branches of a cypress tree, his Kalashnikov rifle cradled in his arms. Paul saw that from his point of advantage Flagstaff could look down into the cabin of the houseboat, and wondered about it. He climbed up the tree, set himself on an adjoining branch, and said, "Anything?"

The Indian shook his head.

"She's got to be here soon."

The Indian nodded. He picked up one of three small pebbles he had put close by in the crotch of the limbs and held it out, saying nothing, then put it down again. Paul looked at it, puzzled for a moment, then realized what the Seminole was implying.

He indicated the rifle, and said, smiling, "Did you steal it from them?"

He nodded, his face very grave and calm.

"Is there anything you want?"

The Indian shook his head. Paul sighed and climbed back down again, and when he entered the cabin, Sarah was lying on the bed, naked, half a torn blanket across her loins. The old man was happily asleep, his ancient body curled up in the sagging chair, a benign smile on his parchment face.

He stood looking down at her. She was lovely, a ragged, unkempt child-woman, warm as an animal. He said, troubled, "This is not really the thing to do, Sarah." He wondered how old she really was.

She was smiling up at him, holding out a grubby hand. "Why not? I want you inside me, and that's where you want to be, I kin tell. Makin' love's always good, the best thing there is, didn't you know that?"

"Melanie might come in"

She was genuinely surprised. "What's that got to do with it? If she wants to watch, I don't care none. I watch her with Flagstaff all the time. Besides, Melanie's too busy keeping watch out there."

"Tell me how old you really are."

"That don't matter none, Paul." She hesitated, and said firmly, "Nineteen."

"Or fifteen?"

"Nineteen, twenty maybe. How should I know? I don't remember when I was born. It was long enough ago, that's all I know." She smiled petulantly. "We bin good to you, Paul, now you be good to me."

She pushed aside the remnant of blanket, took his hand, laid it on her stomach, and said again, pleading, "Be good to me, Paul. Please?"

He leaned forward and kissed her, wondering if the silent Flagstaff were watching through the flimsy drapes of the big, wood-framed window.

And when at last the Indian's pebble landed on the roof of the cabin, he stood up quickly and got back into his clothes. Then Melanie was there, coming in quickly and silently, a finger to her lips, saying, "I seen her, she's coming, way down the path." He handed Sarah her shift; and watched her slip it over her child's body, smiling at him contentedly. He looked at Melanie and sighed, and Melanie laughed suddenly, delighted, and sat down on the other bed to wait.

And then, Carolyne Southby was there.

They felt the boat rocking gently first, and then her shadow was in the doorway, and she was looking round the room in surprise. There was a Kalashnikov machine pistol in her hands, lightly held and not threatening anyone, and she said sharply, looking at Paul, "Who are you?"

He said, standing up, "I'm Paul Tobin. You know the others, I think?"

"Sure I know them. What goes on? I was to meet someone here, Where is he?"

"He's not here."

Now, the gun barrel was raised, and it was pointing straight at him. Paul spread his arms wide. "You don't need that. I'm a friend of Harry's."

"Then where is he? How come I don't know you? I know all of Harry's friends."

He said gently, "Harry doesn't have any friends anymore, Carolyne. He's dead."

He saw her face blanche and knew that Rick's evaluation was correct, that it was going to work. She said angrily, "I don't believe it, I'd have heard..." Her face was still white and she was trembling.

He shook his head. "Put that gun down, for Chrissake, they've got a hair trigger on them."

"First, you tell me. Fast."

"You would not have heard about it. Who from? Simon Kirby? Simon Kirby killed him," Paul replied.

She stared at him, believing, and not believing. Her voice was hoarse. "Why should he do that?"

Paul shrugged: "Harry was in the way. It's pretty simple."

She remembered the coarse hands on her at the motel, the incongruity of the black eye patch between her breasts, the searing violence of his entry. Paul threw himself at her as he saw the trigger finger begin to tense, and when the gun fired, at that precise moment, he was low on the floor. The bullets cut a swathe over his head.

His shoulders made contact with her shins, he threw up an arm and grabbed the gun by its breech, tore it away from her, and felt her teeth sinking into his wrist. She was reaching for the gun again, and he jabbed her quite lightly on the solar plexus. When she doubled up on the ground, rolling over and clutching at her stomach, he stood over her, slipping out the magazine, ejecting the round that was in the breech, and tossing the machine pistol onto the bed.

Sarah and Melanie were on their feet, staring in shock, their hands to their faces in identical positions. The old man had awakened and was climbing to his feet, cold sober again and shouting, "Don't you fire them things in my house!"

"It's all over now," Paul said. He leaned down and helped Carolyne to her feet, "Come with me, I'll take you to his body."

She was limp in his grasp. She whispered, "Who are you?"

"I told you my name. That's all you need to know at the moment."

"Where...where is he?"

"A little way down the creek. I'll show you."

"Show me, then."

"It's not a nice sight, I'm afraid." She was a frightened, helpless child now. How many people had she killed? It was not hard for him to play the part.

"How long has he been...dead?"

"Long enough. Wet ground—it's not good on a body. And he was strangled, wire round his throat." It was Simon Kirby's favorite method, the silent death of the night patrols in Southeast Asia. She nodded and said again, "Show me."

He led her out and the old man followed. But when the girls fell in behind him, he said anxiously; "No, I think you'd better wait for us here..."

Sarah said, "We're coming too, Paul."

He frowned. "You won't like what you see."

And Melanie, too, "We're coming."

He could not insist. Any delay now, he was thinking, and the delicate balance of belief...

They went over the gangplank, a solemn procession of them, making their way through the sludge and the stagnant water of the swamp. When they reached the spot, Flagstaff was there, silent as ever, standing beside an open grave, a long handled shovel in his hand. The body was close by, a blanket over it, and Paul said, "Are you sure?"

Carolyne nodded. There had been tears in her eyes, but they were dry now. She said again, "I want to see..."

At Paul's signal, Flagstaff bent down and pulled away the blanket. She stared at the bloated, blue-black face, swollen and half eaten away, and turned away fast, her hands to her eyes.

The blanket fell back into place quickly, a half second of exposure, no more, and Paul knew that it had worked. His hands were hard on Carolyne's shoulders. The two young girls were clutching at each other, sorry now, perhaps, that they had acquiesced in this terrible thing, not understanding the reason for it, knowing only that other terrible things were happening around the crude animal-lair that had become the only home they had ever known.

Only the old man was unmoved. He stared at the bundle

under the blanket and said, "Was he one o' them Spaniards? I never did think much o' them Spaniards. Ain't no grief seein' another one dead. Why, I recall the day I killed seven of them with my own bare hands, or was it eight?"

Paul nodded to the Indian, "All right, Flagstaff, he's all yours." The Indian put his shovel under the body, levered it into the grave, and began shoveling mud onto it.

The two young girls were staring at Paul. He looked at them and said gravely, "Thank you Sarah, Melanie. Without your help..." To Carolyne he said briefly, explaining it away, "They found the grave."

Without them, he knew, it would not have been so easy. He felt suddenly very angry, looking at the unexpected tears on Sarah's face, seeing the dazed look in Melanie's eyes, feeling the shaking of Carolyne's shoulders against his chest. *That bastard Rick Meyers, he should have seen this through himself*, he thought savagely. And then he understood that his own easy confidence was part of it all too, an essential part of it; and that Rick had known this as well, as Rick knew everything there was to be known about deviousness, and cunning, and sheer bloody devilry.

When Rick Meyers found the answer to a problem, it always worked.

Carolyne Southby said suddenly, looking up at him fiercely, "Are you a cop? I want to talk to a cop."

He shook his head. "Not a cop. But you can talk to me as much as you want. There's a lot I want to hear."

She looked back at the half-covered grave, at Flagstaff stolidly and silently working with his shovel, and said, "How did you find these people? We used them once..."

"Yes, I know." He added sadly, "I use them too. Come. I'll take you to meet some friends."

He watched the family move back toward their ramshackle houseboat, the old man leading the way, moving with practiced ease through the swamp, the two girls behind him. Sarah turned and raised a pathetic hand, and he waved back and waited till they had gone. Then he took Carolyne's arm and led her to where she could do the Private Army the most good.

CHAPTER 9

The Swamp.

Coordinates: 81.17E
              26.13N

Cass Fragonard and Manuel, the Brazilian, had made contact.

All day long the heat had been building up. Now it seemed as though the heavy gray mist that swirled around the trees in unexpected patterns was itself composed of steam. There was mud here to a depth of nearly three feet, a greasy black mud that clung to the legs as a man moved through it, sucking him back as though trying, with a mind of its own, to drag him down to rot in it.

And the two men were playing games with each other.

Four hours earlier they had communicated by their senders, using the UHV waves that had been allotted to them, and now their physical meeting was close at hand. Each of them, quite independently, had decided to test the other's skills.

Manuel was thinking, *With those tin legs, he's not going to be able to climb very well, so I'll take the treetops.* And Cass was saying to himself, *He'll be sure I can't climb trees as well as he can, so that's where he'll be, up top, tout en haut.*

There was one short brush with an alligator, but Cass had

107

heard the swish of the water and was out onto dryer land in a split second, his rifle ready. He saw the great snout, tossed a contemptuous twig at it, and went on his way.

Manuel, clambering from bough to bough, was in his element. In his native Amazon jungle, he would climb any tree as fast as a jaguar, finding handholds and footholds where there were none, swinging his wiry, muscular body along like a monkey, one hand sufficing to bold his weight, the other always searching for newer and higher handholds. He was a legend in his own village, and here, in the angry, alien swamp, the trees were his friends.

Once, a bough broke, rotten to the core, and he crashed twenty feet down into the soft mud, but he was up at the top again within seconds, moving on easily with consummate skill.

And then, he saw them.

He had taken a leap from one cypress to another and was peering darkly at a giant mangrove, searching out the best place to land in it, when he heard the distant sound of a voice. It was an oath, subdued, an angry man cursing the mosquitoes, somebody else, disembodied in the mist, laughed. He heard the changing sound as they moved into deep water, and they were coming his way, perhaps a dozen of them.

He flattened himself against a limb of the tree and waited. Soon he saw them, a line of eleven men and three women, very young people all of them.

(He could not know it, but these youngsters were returning from the task that Simon Kirby had allotted them. The Inter-America Agricultural Alliance was meeting at Key Largo, and the eight cars that were carrying the visitors from Central and South America were to use Highway 1 to take them there from Florida City. Highway 1 had now been mined in fourteen places, three of them with the sophisticated land mines that Carolyne Southby had constructed, their detonators set for eight impacts plus three minutes time-lapse.)

They were joking among themselves as they approached. They were all carrying their Kalashnikov guns, with the habitual grenade around their belts, and one of them was carrying on his shoulders the aluminum case that had held their mines.

(And Manuel could not have known, either, that all these mines had already been defused—an anonymous phone call to the proper quartet. Carolyne Southby's reports were thoroughly detailed.)

He could smell the stench of their sweat as they drew closer. They passed close by beneath him. He moved his head a fraction and watched them work with their machetes, slicing a way through. And when they had been swallowed up in the mist, and the sound of their passing had gone, he took out his chart, studied it, and marked the points on it, with the annotation: *eleven men, three women, 208 degrees, usual weapons, time, 4:35 pm.*

He wondered if he should call Cass on his sender to warn him, and then decided that Cass was perfectly capable of taking care of himself. He moved on, swinging across the boughs, getting closer to the rendezvous coordinates and watching with the utmost care now. He was thinking, *If he sees me before I see him, the indignity of it...*

He found a niche in a fork of the trees, where the moss hung thick and wet, and stared out at the bend in the stream below, which was his pinpoint. He watched every inch of the ground and saw nothing but sludge and sedge and mud and foliage. As he slewed around to examine the ground behind him, something clipped at him through the leaves and snipped sharply into the tree trunk by his head. He looked; a small steel ball was embedded in the thick bark; and then Cass showed himself, grinning and putting away his slingshot. Manuel dropped to the ground beside him, grasped his hand, and said, "You old bastard, you're supposed to be too old for this game, *este jeito...*"

The Frenchman was delighted. He said, happily, "You

goddamn Brazilian monkey, I've been watching you for the last five minutes. Did you see the men?"

Manuel nodded eagerly. "And the women. There was one there with a figure...The one with the long legs, did you see?"

"I saw, of course I saw. I thought of separating her from the others and teaching her that it is better to make love than war. But I subjugated my baser instincts, deciding that next time I see her...Ah yes, those legs..."

"And eyes to make a man lose his mind." Manuel clapped Cass on the shoulder and said; "How are you, you old bastard?"

Cass pulled out his cognac flask and offered it, saying, "As long as I have this, and it is full...My spirits decline as these spirits get lower and lower, but now, my flask is full, and therefore I am a happy man. Show me your map."

They crouched together in the dim light, fast going now, brought out the pencil flashlights, and studied the annotations. Cass said, "Ten hideouts, eight of them manned. And so far...how many men, do you think?"

"At a guess, a hundred and fifty or so. There will be more."

"You heard from Paul?"

"Yesterday, I have to report again at nine tonight."

"Ah, then you don't know. We're almost ready to go."

"Good, I do not like this jungle as much as my own."

"Carolyne Southby has come over to our side. A mine of information. Any day now...the balloons going up."

"And the main force? The rest of the boys?"

Cass shrugged. "Who knows? Only Paul, and Rick, and Bramble. They say Pamela Charles will come with the Colonel again. And Betty de Haas too."

"Ah, Betty de Haas...Just the sight of her body drives me mad. Have you ever seen her naked?"

Cass nodded. "Once. When she was swimming with the Colonel. It's not often I envy other men, but then...Yes, I envied him."

He was looking older tonight, Manuel thought, and small wonder. In the last five days, Cass Fragonard had covered more than a hundred and fifty miles of the swampland, moving back and forth in a crisscross pattern, pushing himself hard for twelve or thirteen hours a day, resting at nightfall and off again as soon as there was enough light. Manuel touched the map with a hairy finger. Some of the strongpoints were marked in red, some in blue, and only three of them in yellow. He said: "Yellow, Efrem Collas, he hasn't found very much, has he?"

"Efrem was pulled out. I took over his area."

"It is a great advantage to have tin legs, they don't get tired. As for me, I could do with ten days of sleep in a good bed, with the long-legged terrorist girl beside me for comfort. How can a woman as beautiful as she is kill as easily as these people do, can you answer me that?"

"One day, perhaps, we will ask her. Now, the target..."

Manuel looked at the map, checked his compass, and pointed. "There, forty-three degrees precisely, for two miles. A nighttime operation, in this God-forsaken place..."

"The night will make it easy for us to get away. Have you seen it close up?"

"Very close."

"Then you must guide me in. I have only a map reference."

"I wonder how many people will be there?"

Cass raised an elegant shoulder. "Does it matter? Six rounds from each of us and there will be nothing left."

It was Major Bramble's instruction.

On the master chart, one of the identified strongholds seemed to the cursory glance to be out of kilter with what he fondly called "their thin red line."

He had said, drawing his finger from one point to another, "You see what they've done? If you take into account the contours here and here, and the two streams that run across here, what they've really done is build a defensive line which they can hold from both sides. At first glance, it all looks a little haphazard, doesn't it, but we have to bear one thing in mind: Kirby's a highly trained jungle fighter, and he's built himself a line he can hold. All of Strickland's past forays into the swamp should have taught him that too, but it seems they didn't, and I think I know why."

He was off on one of his favorite subjects, the lesson he called "knowing your enemy." He sat back and said, "With all of Kirby's past very carefully annotated, Strickland still didn't realize that he's a born strategist, and a man like that is just not capable, when it comes to a fight, of setting out his forces incorrectly. Everything in Kirby's military past points to one thing—his instinct for tactics, which is superb. So I looked for some kind of method in his placing of these strongpoints, and by God, I found it."

Bramble stabbed at the chart again: "Follow the contours, Paul. Look for the natural obstacles, and there's his line. But the one we call Stronghold Eight, sticking out like a sore thumb on the flank, serves a vital purpose: it provides covering fire. The only way you can get at his line, the only feasible route in, you're vulnerable to Eight long before you get there. It's the best hidden of all of them, and Strickland almost certainly never knew it was there."

Paul studied the annotations, knowing that Bramble was right. He stood up and paced the crow's nest for a while, watching Rena at work with her camera, admiring the slim lines of her young body, wondering if she was up to the dangerous task ahead of her.

He turned back to Bramble. "All right. Eight will have to be knocked out."

"And soon. Before we start the main attack."

"But not too soon. We don't want to give him a chance to rebuild it."

"No, Paul. He won't rebuild it. Number Eight's strength lies largely in its concealment. Once he finds out that it's been discovered, he'll know the position has lost its usefulness."

Paul thought about it for a while. He nodded, and said, "All right, I'll buy that. We'd better check with Rick."

Bramble said happily, his battle won, "I did that already. Rick agrees with me. He says knock it out as soon as you can."

"Then that's what we'll do." He smiled at the eager look on Major Bramble's face, "And then, I take it, we'll be ready to go?"

Bramble nodded. "As soon as the Colonel gives the word."

"I'll check with him. We're counting heavily on Kirby and all his men being just where we hope they are."

"Yes. But that's where Rena comes in, isn't it?"

He had hated the idea at first; now that Rick had explained it to him, defined the security measures that were to be taken, he was learning to live with it. But he looked across at her and said, "But if they as much as lay a hand on you, I'll personally break every bone in Rick Meyer's body."

She was sitting in the corner, quietly photographing with the little Minox the thick bundle of shorthand pages she had taken down as Paul had questioned Carolyne Southby. Carolyne herself was close beside her, still in a state of semi-shock but slowly coming out of it.

Her mind was still filled with hatred, a fierce hatred of Simon Kirby; soon she would begin to question her actions, and then that hatred would become dangerous. But for the moment, she sat there staring at them blankly, knowing that something had happened that was far beyond her comprehension, knowing that all was not really as it seemed to be.

"Rena, get on the blower for me, will you?" Paul said. "I want to speak to the Colonel."

The two men studied the stronghold in the evening light.

Stronghold Eight was a long, low building, half submerged below ground level and built of heavy wooden slabs that had been covered over—to a depth of more than two feet—with a tangle of living vines and sedge. Only the footsteps in the wet mud, harder to pick out now in the semidarkness even with the powerful glasses, gave any evidence at all that there was something there other than virgin forest.

Cass pointed. There was a sentry stationed close by the hidden entrance, a solitary man in camouflage uniform, with twigs and small branches tied to his helmet, the muzzle of his gun protruding through the leaves of the sheltering bushes. The two hidden men, a silent, prowling unseen menace, watched as he moved his head slowly, the dark eyes searching and finding nothing.

Manuel took out his slingshot and gestured with it, raising his eyebrows. Cass shook his head. He put his lips close to the Brazilian's ear and whispered, "No chance of a clean shot, forget it." He touched the stock of his Carlson, and pointed again. "There, to the left, get up in the big mangrove tree. I'll give you ten minutes. When you hear my first round, start firing."

Manuel slipped away. Watching him go and hearing no sound at all, Cass thought, *He moves like a snake in the mud a moccasin gliding silently, and just as deadly.*

He waited. The Carlson gun was ready.

He had changed to the alternate breech and had slipped in the magazine of pencil grenades, the long slim packets of high explosive with their sharp, carbon-steel points. He had set their timers for two seconds, and two seconds after impact they would explode like bazooka shells, only ten times as deadly. Under the tiny detonator was a potent mixture of TNT, with PETN and Cyclonite added.

He scraped carefully and silently at the wet earth under him, watching the sentry all the time, digging himself in to avoid, for as long as he could, the shock of his own explosives. He always pretended it gave him a headache.

He checked the range carefully with his finder—one hundred and eighty-five yards. Manuel would be a little closer, and higher too, firing down into the roof.

He waited.

The minute hand of his watch moved on. He adjusted his position carefully and set the slim barrel of the Carlson on the mound of earth in front of him. There was just enough light, no more.

He fired.

The red tracer told him it had struck home, and instinctively he ducked, waiting for the blast. When it came, he felt the wind whistling over his head as fragments of wood clipped their way out into the tightly packed vegetation. He fancied he heard a scream, and fired again, two shots in rapid succession, then ducked down again as the blast hit him.

Now Manuel was firing methodically too, the red line of the shells coming from high, very high up in the mangrove and beating down into the timber roof.

There was no sense now in concealment. He stood up and, bracing himself against the blast, fired three more times, a round at each end of the building—what was left of it—and the final round in the center. As the sound of the last explosion died down, he crouched onto his metal heels and waited again.

There was fire there now—the interior of the stronghold was burning fast. Manuel came at a run, saying, "Well, let's get over there..."

Cass shook his head. "Down, down, we don't know

what's in there."

Manuel crouched: "Then let's go find out."

Cass laid a restraining hand on his arm. "No, we wait."

In a moment, the secondary explosions began, a series of short, sharp blasts at one end of the wreckage, and Manuel said, grinning, "I see what you mean."

And then, as they watched, a storage room for explosives blasted its way out into the surrounding trees, shattering their trunks with the immensity of its fury. The swamp was filled with the angry roar of it, and red and yellow flames shot high up into the overhanging canopy, spewing out smoke and refuse and burning woodwork, sending the great timbers high into the air, twisting and turning over and over as the force of the blast sledgehammered the two men deep into the mud.

Manuel said, "Christ, what have they got in there?"

Cass grimaced. "Nothing, not anymore."

Pieces of charred timbers were raining down beside them. A burning beam fell across Cass's legs, burning his trousers. He rolled out from under it and said, grinning, "You see? A flesh and blood leg would have been broken. Me, need only a soldering iron..."

It was a raging furnace over there now. Cass took out his sender and threw the switch to his wavelength. "Paul? Rick? Come in please."

He was plugging in the tiny earphone when the voice came to him, "Bramble here, Cass, go ahead."

"Stronghold Eight destroyed, Major Bramble," Cass said happily. "Nothing left of it at all."

"Good. Are you both all right? Any problems?"

"Manuel is in love with a terrorist girl. Because of her legs."

Bramble said patiently, "Sergeant Fragonard, do you have any casualties to report?"

"One tin leg bent out of shape, Major, but nothing I can't

fix with a hammer."

"Good. We need both of you back at H.Q. Get on over here. Out"

Cass put the sender away in its case at his hip, and they moved off together through the dank morass of the swamp. The fire was still raging behind them, and they could still feel its frightening heat. Cass was moving awkwardly, swinging his twisted leg out and around into position again. In a little while he said, "*Merde!* We take a workshop break, Manuel."

Manuel squatted down and watched as Cass took off his leg, found a suitable stone, and hammered the metal straight again. He connected it up, tried it out, and said happily, "There, you see? As good as new."

The darkness swallowed them up.

CHAPTER 10

Shark River.

Coordinates: 81.21E
                      25.72N

Twenty-one miles north of Ponce de Leon Bay, where the Shark River winds its forlorn way into the Everglades, the Private Army of Colonel Tobin was landing under cover of a darkness that was absolute.

A body of highly armed aliens was splashing ashore from the rubber boats, setting foot for the first time on American soil, a small, tightly knit band of the best fighting men in the world.

Half a mile to the west, a splendid ocean-going yacht, the personal property of Colonel Tobin's man in the Caribbean, was standing at anchor in the shallows, its dark blue hull invisible, its lights all extinguished, and the voices aboard controlled and muffled.

It had brought the men from Cabo Isabella, in the Dominican Republic, where, by devious arrangements with the Dominican Government (or more specifically, with some of its more venal officials), they had landed forty-two hours earlier, together with all their weapons and their heavy crates of supplies.

This in itself had been no mean endeavor.

Their 747, owned and operated by the Colonel and flown

by his best pilot, young Moretti, had carried them out to Dominica, cleared at London's Gatwick airport as a load of tourists. The weapon cases were labeled "Farm Equipment, Property of the Office for Overseas Development". The plane had landed at night on the airstrip west of Santiago Rodriguez. They boarded the waiting trucks and were quickly carried down to the coast, where other anxious officials were waiting to shepherd them aboard the yacht and get them out of the country—before some Minister might hear about this flagrant breach of sovereign rights.

The yacht was a beautiful vessel, called the *Maya*. Her immense twin Diesels and close to 16,000 feet of sail could carry her along at about thirty knots. She had covered the seven hundred and forty miles in a little over thirty-two hours, close in off Cuba's shoreline (where she had been harried by the coastal guns firing hopefully across her bows), past the southern tip of Andros Island, through the Marquesas Keys and the Dry Tortugas, and straight in on a rapid course of forty-seven to Shark Island and the Shark River. Here she had turned northwest and cruised quietly along the coast, an innocent vessel searching for a suitable harbor. Her Captain had timed the arrival, at a point seven and one-quarter miles south-southeast of Pavilion Key, for one hour after the set of the moon, or two-forty-five in the morning.

The waters were calm and dark and silent. Far out in the Gulf, a liner was steaming slowly past, far away on the horizon. A plane flew high in the night sky, heading for Venezuela.

Each rubber boat, pushing its way through the dense masses of kelp, had a solitary seaman, who would paddle it back for reloading on board the yacht after his complement had been landed under the watchful eye of Captain Duyvel, the Beach Master. He was urging them up the beach now, into the swamp, and on to the staging area where Rick Meyers was waiting to guide them. They would be hidden around the swamps, in twos and threes, one hundred men in contact with their Squad Commanders on their own individual senders, the Commanders with theirs for communication with H.Q.

They would hide and wait, unseen and unheard, until it was time for them to rise up out of the ground, like ghouls.

There were one hundred alien soldiers here, on American soil, dressed in their jungle green-and-gray, armed to the teeth with their deadly Carlson guns, their commando brass-knuckled knives, and—some of them—with the silent and highly efficient bows of English yew with their Fort Oxford cedar shafts from Formosa.

One hundred alien troops—and no one was aware of their coming.

Duyvel whispered, "Hurry it up now, Roberts, get your squad under cover, you think the Coast Guard isn't prowling around out there? Looking for us?"

"Hell, Captain, don't rush me, I got a hernia," Roberts quipped.

Hanson was single-handedly hoisting a massive crate onto his back, staggering under its weight. He was a huge man, a fine athlete, and he'd lost a hunk of meat out of his shoulder a while back, to a mortar fragment. There was Gopa, the Nepalese, Ghurka from Katmandu, a slight dark, and muscular man who could have passed for a Seminole himself.

There was Edgars Jefferson, the giant black man from Chicago who had been beaten and thrown into a stockade in Vietnam for his part in a mutiny, which, in Colonel Tobin's opinion, had been not only justified but necessary.

He was the Private Army's best weapons man, a Specialist, a technician of the highest order. If you gave Edgars Jefferson the most sophisticated weapon just off the classified list, he would strip it down to its last nut or bolt and rebuild it, making it twice as good and ten times as deadly. He was a genius.

There was Sergeant Miguel Sampaio, and Ramatul Singh the Sikh, and Ahmed Idriss, the Senussi archer who had once been instructor to the family of the late King Said Idriss of Libya. Ahmed, without doubt the best bowman in the world, was wrapped in his Bedouin *jurd*, the long cloak of camels hair that served as a blanket, a cloak, or merely, as now, to announce to the world that he was a Senussi.

There was Asa, the Yemeni Jew, with his close friend and fellow Yemeni, Yehud; and Carlo, the elderly Cuban, the oldest man in the Private Army and the one who moved in the deepest silence; and Tosa Satsym the Japanese, the best underwater man who had ever lived; and the Mexican, Mendoza; and Hamash, the Turk, who had lost a foot in the Dead Sea battle. Hamash was now a close friend of Cass Fragonard, the two of them walking on metal.

There was Alaric, the cool, silent Icelander from Reykjavik, a long, lean and scrawny man; and Romulo from Buenos Aires; and Pastroudis the Greek ex-bandit, a flowery man with a huge black moustache and a penchant for pinching the women's behinds, any woman's...

And there was Rudi Vicek, head of communications, a man who could talk in six different codes on six different channels at the same time on the highly sophisticated, immensely intricate computer-radio-scanner which he had designed, perfected, and built himself, a man who had devoted all his studies to one thing, and to one thing only—the science of communicating with distant bodies.

When he had made his latest modifications, he had patted the beloved console as though it were made of female flesh, and had said, "With this...Put a man in a submarine at the bottom of the Mariana Trench, and with this I'll monitor his heartbeat for you. Let him land on the moon, and I'll tell you when he takes a crap. Lock him up in a lead lined room, and I'll still take his photograph for you..."

Reddigan, Santi Smith, Brennan, Vissela, Kasvin, all the others were there. They had come from all over the world from all walks of life and from all shades of the political spectrum; they were of all ages and races and philosophies. Only one thing held them together—the knowledge that now they were serving in the toughest little army in the world.

They were all here now, all moving into position, turning back to watch the black boats and the white surf, and knowing that, for them, the excitement was soon to begin.

They moved quickly off the beach, all of them save Duyvel, and disappeared into the darker depths of the swamp.

Duyvel switched on his sender. "All men landed, Skipper, all supplies ashore, last dinghy returning now," he said quietly.

"Good," replied the Skipper; a gruff, old sailing man from New England. "About time. The Coast Guard'll be finding me any minute now if I don't get out of here. And then, what's the Colonel going to have to say, can you tell me that? Good luck, Duyvel."

The Captain switched off. He took a last, long and careful look around the beach. The tide was coming in and would soon wash away their footprints. He listened for a while for any sound. There was none. He turned and followed the others into the swamp, his illuminated compass in his hand, his Carlson gun over his shoulder.

He wondered how long he'd have to sit there, cooped up in a heavily camouflaged pup-tent in the mud, waiting for the fighting to start. Tomorrow the long, long trek through the Everglades would begin, fifty-seven miles of sludge, mud, and mosquitoes.

In the damp darkness he thought, *Surely no place on earth can be as God-forsaken as this!*

But when the dawn came and he stretched his cramped legs, saw the early-morning gold on the mist, the yellow-green moss hanging down, and the stark, dramatic tangle of the trees, he thought, *It's the night that makes all things evil, and the sun that brings us...this kind of beauty.*

Another somber group of armed men was moving through the early-morning fog.

There were twenty-seven of them, men and women assorted, and they wore the uniforms that Simon Kirby had insisted they wear in the swamps, under which were the jeans and shirts they would wear for their appointed tasks.

They were heading for the track that ran along the canal where it twisted southwest and then northwest again, where the trucks would be waiting, two farm trucks and a pick-up.

The trucks would take them to Naples, Fort Myers, and Punta Gorda, dropping them off at chosen intervals with their loads of high explosives and their Kalashnikov rifles. From here, they would spread out, individually or in small groups, each to his or her allotted task.

At Fort Myers, a Russian ballet company was to perform that night. Three of the Algerian contingent of the CAAA were to explode three napalm bombs, stolen from the arsenal in Tampa, in the theater. It was hoped that at least some of the Russians would be killed.

In Naples, the Israeli Emergency Protection League was meeting to consolidate its Florida operations; the meeting place was to be blown up. At that precise moment—Kirby was a stickler for timing—the two representatives of the Palestinian Assistance League, who were soliciting funds there, were to be assassinated. In Punta Gorda, where the World Health Organization was debating the question of supplying the new "super rice" to Southeast Asia, the meeting place was to be firebombed. Twelve letter-bombs were to be posted along the way, to carefully selected recipients. The Fire Department's new building at Bayshore was to be blown up, and the new bridge over the Caloosahatchee River at Olga was to be destroyed with eleven pounds of TNT.

Two men—Suleiman Descartes, the fanatical Algerian, and Roland Watt, a black from Washington—together with a tough and bitter young woman, Annie Gorusia from Ohio, were to hijack the Pan Am plane scheduled to leave Fort Myers at midday for West Palm Beach and Miami. They had been ordered to demand half a million dollars for its ransom. Each of them was carrying one letter-bomb, a thin sheet of plastic explosive in an ordinary (opened, stamped, and worn) air mail envelope, plus one tiny plastic single-shot pistol made up to look like a Bic ballpoint pen. These had been made in Japan and had no range or velocity at all. But they were made for a specific purpose: with the point of the pen held against the victim's neck, a push on the pocket clip would, at such close range, blow a hole the size of a golf ball in the victim's throat.

The letter-bombs needed no metallic detonator; a modicum of pressure on their flat surface was enough to blow everything within a fifty-foot range to smithereens. These had been made in Libya by the organization that was supplying the Black September group, and four hundred and fifty of them had been bought by Kirby from the Consolidated Interfield Arms Company of Birmingham, Alabama.

It was one of the little quirks that lay on the periphery of any operation like Simon Kirby's; Consolidated Interfield was owned and operated by the CIA, though Kirby could never have come to learn this. As for Consolidated, they could never have known that the checks issued to them on a numbered Swiss bank account, ostensibly serving a group in Libya dedicated to the overthrow of that country's virulent and unpredictable Marxist dictator, were in fact coming from another group that was seeking the overthrow of Chile's leftist government, or that behind them there was yet another group of dedicated, apolitical, and quite amoral financiers who were only interested in the profits; and finally, that behind *them*, there was Kirby.

The arms would be shipped from port to port, from country to country, but always, only on paper. In effect, they were sent from the Company's warehouses in Birmingham to Mobile, where waiting trucks would take them away, no questions asked.

Why should there be questions? By now, one Swiss bank had made a transfer of funds to another Swiss bank, and that was all that mattered.

The column of deadly, fanatical terrorists moved on through the swamp, in single file, led by Simon Kirby himself. He was in a violent rage at the unexplained disappearance of Carolyne Southby; and he was worried about Harry Dewitt.

He had called Washington that morning. He had said, "Dewitt? Is Carolyne with you?"

He had tried to evaluate the hesitation at the other end. "Carolyne? No, she's not here, I thought she was still with you."

"Well, she's not. She's split."

Harry said firmly, "Then she's been picked up."

"If she had, I'd have heard about it, one way or another."

"Maybe that's true, maybe not. But they can't hold her, Kirby, not for long."

"Major."

"Yes, sir, Major Kirby. Like I was saying, if they've picked her up, what are they going to do with her? She won't talk, you know that."

"No, I know that. But I still don't like it. I don't like the silence."

"The silence?"

"There's a news blackout on everything relating to us. Something's in the wind, and I don't like it. You'd better get back here, Dewitt, I've an idea they'll be coming at us again, maybe in force this time, and I want every available man in position. This could be it, Harry. The big or one."

"Let's be ready for it."

"Okay, Major."

"If you hear anything about Carolyne, I want to know right away."

"Okay."

Now he was fuming still. He fell back as the column began to move into more open country and waited for Annie Gorusia to catch up. She was fourteenth down the line and would head the group that moved west when they split up, three miles from here. When she came up, he said, "Wait a minute, Annie..."

The men behind her slipped under cover and waited.

She sat on the ground behind him and locked her arms around her knees, a twenty-four-year-old, not unattractive woman, except for that bitter, sullen mouth. Over her long skirt, tied up now round her waist, and her tank top, she wore the camouflage uniform, open at the neck, with her unruly hair piled up under the beret.

"I don't want any mistakes on this one, Annie," Kirby said; "You've got to keep an eye on Descartes—he gets too goddamned excited too easily. Hold him in check. It's the co-pilot or the navigator he's got to go for, not the pilot. I don't want that plane to crash while you're still on it. Just lay your letter-bombs around, very gently, where someone is sure to see them, pick them up. All they need is a touch..."

She was very calm about it. "Descartes is willing to stay on board, did you know that? To make sure of it."

He was not really surprised. Watching her face closely, he said; "He'll back out at the last moment. I know the type."

"No, he won't. A hundred-odd passengers on board, a five-million-dollar plane...He wants to head out over the Caribbean as soon as Roland Watt and I have jumped, tell them he's making for Cuba. He wants to feel the power of it in his hands just as long as he can stand it, and then step on the bombs, on all of them."

Kirby wondered if he really needed Descartes any longer. He weighed the relative values and said, "You get the ransom money at Fort Lauderdale, together with six parachutes, two for each of you. They just might try and shoot your tires out again."

She shook her head. "No...There was too much of an outcry the last time."

"True...You'll have to play it cool all the way. If they suspect..."

He thought about it, frowning, and said at last, "Not Cuba. Cuba's getting tough with the hijackers now, and the pilot will wonder how come Descartes doesn't know that. I don't want him wondering about anything, just a normal hijacking, a smooth, easy operation. Have him say Haiti—it makes more sense. You're sure he'll do it?"

"He'll do it. He's waiting for you to tell him to do it."

"Then get him over here."

She stood up and walked back, and in a moment she returned with Descartes beside her. She had already told him; there was a strange and jubilant light in those black and piercing eyes. He stood like a restless animal, half prowling, his weight constantly shifting from one leg to another.

"So you're going to kill yourself off, Descartes, is that it?" Kirby asked.

His eyes were on fire, "Yes, I kill myself off. One hundred passengers, maybe more, maybe a lot more..."

"Only when the others are safely out."

"I know that."

"You kill the navigator or the co-pilot first, to make sure they go along with what Annie tells them to do. And you don't say head for Cuba, you make it Haiti, you understand?"

"Haiti?"

"Haiti. It's important."

"Haiti then. I tell them first they're all going to die. I want to see their faces."

"Tell them what you goddam please—just make sure you don't back out at the last moment. I don't want you locked up in Haiti, or anywhere else. You know too much about us."

"Ha! You don't realize, Major, I am an Algerian—I am not afraid to die" He squatted on his heels suddenly, laid a hand on Kirby's knee, and said excitedly, "You know? Palm Beach, Miami, half the passengers, maybe more, maybe all of them...They will be Jews, you realize that?"

Kirby said gravely, "Almost certain to be, Descartes. But remember, Haiti."

Descartes shot out a hand, and Kirby, surprised, took it and held it. He said: "The Muslims...they don't call it Nirvana, do they?"

The Algerian was smiling now, and there were tears in his eyes, a volatile, emotional man with mass murder on his mind. "The Koran tells us, we go to Paradise..." He was still gripping Kirby's hand, and Kirby was beginning to feel uncomfortable. He let it go at last and stood up, saying, "You will tell Black September what I have done?"

"I will tell all of them. I'll make sure they know. Go to it, Descartes."

The Algerian, a jubilant man, moved away and was gone, under cover again in the luxuriant bushes, dreaming of Paradise.

Annie said, "You see the kind of fanaticism these people have?" And Kirby answered her, "That's why they're here, Annie. That's why, I brought them over."

He was thinking of Carolyne, worrying about her and yet wishing he could get his hands on her again. Even though she had been cold and unwilling, there had been a subtle satisfaction in that white, delicate flesh.

He looked at Annie Gorusia and thought, *Christ, what a dog.*

The column moved on. The trucks were waiting at their ordained positions. Kirby watched his commandos climb aboard.

When the trucks had lumbered off along the muddy road that led to the highway, he turned and made his way back to the swamp.

Half a mile down the road, fifteen minutes later, a motorcycle roared to sudden life. Rick Meyers was forcing a Honda through the bushes and over the deeply rutted track. He followed the tracks in the mud till they reached the deserted road, and saw that the vehicles had turned west. He got off his bike, sat in the saddle, and took out his sender.

"Paul? Bram? Come in, please."

It was Rena Susac on the console. She said, her voice soft and feminine, "They're both out, Rick. Shall I get one of them for you?"

"No. Just pass on the message. Twenty-seven men and women, coordinates 198-849, three truckloads all headed west at the moment. It looks like Carolyne's Plan Exeter. Paul might want to make sure they're acting on our information. This is very definite confirmation."

"It's all been done, Rick. Fort Myers, Naples, Punta Gorda, all the others...The FBI's been tipped off, the local police, the sheriff's office...They'll all be out in force, waiting."

"Good. Strike twenty-seven members of the CAAA. But pass on the warnings again, say something like...All twenty-seven terrorists are now en route to their targets, as specified in the last report, something like that. Use your own discretion. I'm particularly worried about that hijacking. Make sure they know the hijackers are carrying the light-touch explosives. One or two of these people just might be suicidal. Make sure they understand that."

"Will do."

"Tell Paul what you've done."

"Will do. Your destination?"

He said softly, "Coming over to see you, Rena. Be there in four hours. Out."

He put away his sender, bullied the bike into the

shrubbery again, and hid it carefully when it could go no further. The rest was footwork, slogging through the mud and the slime on a compass bearing, cutting his way through the barrier of the undergrowth, struggling through the groping mangrove roots that spread their black, unyielding tentacles to prohibit his progress.

He wished there was time to take a bath; he could even smell his own stench.

And eight hours later, twenty-seven members of the CAAA, twenty-one men and six women, were safely under lock and key in the jails of Fort Myers, Naples, and Punta Gorda. Flight 887 from Fort Myers had taken off without incident and had landed safely at its destination.

No one on board had the slightest suspicion of the closeness of sudden death; it had simply passed them all by.

CHAPTER 11

Frogleg Creek.

Coordinates: 81.06E
              26.12N

"There's just too much going on around here that I don't understand. There's too much I don't like," Kirby said.

He stood at the entrance to the houseboat's cabin, his back turned to the interior, not watching what was going on there. He heard Old-Man moaning faintly and was surprised that neither of the girls was screaming.

Bjelovaci the Serb stood by the gangplank, his rifle at the ready, his thick, stubby legs planted firmly on the deck. He shrugged his massive shoulders. "We will find out. It will not take long."

There were two other men there, black men—Randy Shuter and another known only as Clay. They were at the big window, staring out into the swamp, turning from time to time to watch the others.

Kirby turned and looked at Old Man. His wrists and ankles had been tied, and a young woman was turning a wire tourniquet round his forehead, cutting into the fragile flesh over his temples. His face was twisted with pain, and there was a sobbing sound coming from his mouth. The saliva was trickling down over the skeletal jawbone, and his eyes were closed.

The young woman was named Maria Abbyad, and she came from Beirut, a graduate of the American University there, a student, once, of political science. There was an ornate gold crucifix hanging on a thin gold chain at her neck, and as she twisted the twig that tightened the tourniquet, she said savagely, "Talk, damn your eyes, or I kill you..."

He could only moan.

The two girls, Melanie and Sarah, were seated awkwardly on one of the beds, back to back with their wrists tied together, their legs spread out uncomfortably, twisted up underneath their bodies; there was a wire around their two necks, holding them together.

Kirby went over to them and squatted on the ground beside the bed, crouched down on his heels. "He'll die, you know. He'll die soon if someone doesn't talk," he said quietly.

Melanie was trembling, not with fear or pain, but with fury; she was a savage. She spat at him. "Like this, you don't get told nothin', *Nothin'!*"

He wiped the spittle from his face and jerked a thumb at the case of Irish whiskey. "Like that, then? That's not the way I operate, and believe me, my way is more certain."

He went over and took out one of the bottles, tossed it in his hand as though weighing it, and said, "You bribe a man in these parts, you give him bathtub gin, or moonshine, maybe spend a couple of bucks and get him some half-good sour mash. But Irish whiskey? Nobody in these parts uses it. I wonder where it came from? What was there, a whole case? It looks that way, doesn't it? Who uses Irish whiskey around here?"

He signaled the Arab girl, and she twisted the wire tighter. Looking at Melanie he said again, "Who gave him the Irish whiskey, Melanie? Sarah?"

The old man was stuttering, trying to say something. Maria Abbyad relaxed the pressure a trifle, and he said, stammering, his voice very hoarse with his pain, "Remember...remember..."

He broke off, and Kirby asked impatiently, "Remember what, you goddam bastard?"

The ancient eyes, pale and bloodshot now, were on the girls. "Remember what...what I told you...You don't say *nothin'*."

Marin Abbyad pulled tight on the wire again, and he gasped. There were tears in Sarah's eyes, and she screamed out, "No, no, no!"

Kirby reached over and pushed the Arab girl away. "You stupid bitch, you're going to kill him. I want him alive! I told you..."

The old man kneeled over. Kirby swung him around savagely so that he could watch, went over to the two girls, and angrily ripped the cloth dresses from their young bodies. He strode to the gangplank and yelled out, "Scotty! Carlos! Wolfmann! Who's got the whip?"

There were ten men out there in the swamp, tightly concealed among the mangrove roots, their Kalashnikovs on their shoulders, waiting and watching. One of them came running in, Wolfmann the Austrian, who had killed eight American soldiers, a bomb blast, in his native Vienna. He tossed a long, plaited whip to Kirby and hurried back to his post.

Kirby went into the cabin and said, "Now watch, Old Man."

He brought the lash down savagely across Melanie's back, opening up a large, red cut; the tip of it snaked around and sliced a living weal on Sarah's stomach. He raised it again and cut her across the full breast. As he raised the lash a third time, the Old Man shouted, "No...Wait..."

Kirby let his arm drop. He said, very clearly, "I want to know who it was blew up that place of mine by the creek. It wasn't Strickland, for sure. I know you must have guided them there, you or the girls, and I want to know, Old Man. I want to know now."

The old man was silent, his eyes closed. The Arab girl put her wire around his head again, and the old man keeled over and fell to the floor. She bent down to yank him up again and said disgustedly, "He's dead."

Kirby came over and kicked at the body brutally, saying to Randy Shuter, "Throw it into the water—let him rot there." He laughed shortly. "The gators can get their revenge on him—he's eaten enough of them in his time."

He went back to the girls again and showed them the whip, a short, stubby handle of leather-covered rosewood and a six-foot lash. He held it out and said, "How much of this do you think you can survive? It kills, you know. It kills."

He began whipping them again, and they fell sideways on the bed, screaming. In a few moments he undid the wire from their throats, separated them, and said, "I want to know who they're sending after me. I want to know who they are and all about them. It's not the Feds, and it's not the State Police, and it's not the National Guard...So who is it?"

Melanie whimpered, choking. He saw that Sarah had fallen to the floor, unconscious. He lifted her bloodied, naked body in his arms and turned to Melanie, "Melanie?" he said, quite gently. "Can you hear me? If you don't tell me what I want to know, I'm going to stomp her brains out and toss her into the swamp."

He held Sarah's limp body out, and said, "Take a last look, Melanie." She was still choking, fighting for breath, sick with the pain.

Kirby put Sarah back on the floor, close to the bed, put his heavy boot on her groin, and twisted it around. "Fifteen years old, and she's as good as dead." He raised a boot over her face, and Melanie screamed, a long drawn, anguished scream that seemed to reverberate against the solid barrier of living green that was the swamp.

He stood there for a moment, his foot poised, holding on to the edge of the table to keep his balance, and he said, raising his voice over the sound of hers, "Does that mean yes? Or no? What is it, Melanie, it's your last chance."

She was gasping, broken. "They call it...they call it a Private Army. A man named...named Colonel...Colonel Tobin..."

He stood there, staring at her.

And then the sound of the shot came, sudden and unexpected, a sharp, incisive sound that did not come from one of the Kalashnikovs out there. Frozen, he stood there, a statue, his head turned to look at the entrance.

He saw Bjelovaci crumple as the bullet took him through the throat. Then all of them were grabbing for their rifles and throwing themselves out through the door, crouching down in the scuppers and peering out into the swamp.

Randy Shuter, pointing, said, "There, over there by the cypress..." A second bullet opened up his throat and he fell.

Shouting, "With me!" Kirby threw himself backwards over the side of the houseboat and into the water. Clay leaped after him, only to be cut down by the third bullet, which broke his spine at the neck. The body fell into the scuppers and lay there, the head almost severed at the neck.

Maria Abbyad was crouched in the cabin, up against the door, her rifle ready, a grenade in her hand. She pulled the pin with her teeth and tossed it to the shore, throwing it as far as she could. Almost before the explosion had ripped open the greenery, she was running out onto the deck, slipping quickly and expertly under the overhang of the wheelhouse, dragging a heavy crate quickly in behind her to shield her from this angle.

The swamp was silent now, but only momentarily.

She heard the chatter of a machine pistol, and then another. When they fell silent, there were two quick shots with that strangely muted, yet still incisive sound. Someone screamed.

The strange gun fired again, and then again.

She was gauging the position of it, first here, and then there, and she wondered if it was one gun, of were there several? She hurled two more grenades out there, but then the gun sounded again behind her, and she swung round and sought new cover.

The Kalashnikovs were firing again. She heard one of the men—was it young Jimmy Saticoy—shouting, "Over there, over there..." She heard the sound of men crashing through the undergrowth, and somebody screamed as another single shot sounded.

There was silence again. She waited a long, long time, till her patience ran out, and then doubled up and ran quickly to the other end of the deck, crouching down under cover and peering out. Her heart was beating fast, but she was not afraid. She was thinking, *One man out there, maybe two. That's all it is, and I'm better than any man...*

She raised her rifle and pumped twelve shots, very rapidly, into the trees, then slipped in a new magazine and waited. In a little while she tossed another two grenades out there and crawled carefully back toward the cabin. She saw the broken body of the black man, Clay. Looking out across the water, she knew that Kirby had found safety on the other side. Then she looked back to where the shots had come from and wondered why he had stopped shooting...

Suddenly there was a wiry, immensely strong arm around her throat, pulling her in tight, half strangling her. There was a steel hand crushing her arm, not at the gun hand but at the bicep, digging into it so hard that she screamed and dropped her rifle— the arm was paralyzed, completely. Now the arm was gone from her neck and a hand was twisted in her long black hair, wrenching her around and forcing her to the ground, slipping on her knees and being held there. Her left arm was twisted up around her back, and she heard the sickening sound as it pulled out of its socket, felt the intense pain of it shooting down through her body, down to her feet and up again to the top of her head. She was gasping.

Paul Tobin said, very quietly, "How many more of them?"

He was tight against the bulkhead, his body sheltered by its timbers, the gun, of a kind she had never seen before, close by his hand. He dropped her broken arm, took up the gun, gestured with it, and said easily, "I can blow the top of your head off without thinking twice about it."

She shuddered. "No one else."

Could he believe her? He thought perhaps not. He let her fall to the deck. As she went down, he hit her once, expertly and hard, with the flat of his hand just above and behind the ear. He did not wait for the body to slump down, but was in the cabin with a single short run, his back to the wall there and his gun ready. He saw the two girls and said tightly, "How many, Melanie, quickly..."

She twisted her body over, falling to the floor, and gasped, "Two black men, and one other, and Kirby—some more out there in the swamp—I don't know how many."

"Where's Old Man?"

"He's dead there in the water..."

He swore. "Can you walk?"

He unsheathed the bush knife at his waist, its carbon edge honed to perfection. He sliced through the ropes at her wrist, dropped the knife to her, and stood back, waiting. There was no sound out there among the trees. When she was free and had dragged herself painfully across the floor to cut Sarah's bonds too; he asked, "Can you carry her?"

"Yes. I can manage."

"Through the window then, into the water and across the other side, under cover as fast as you can. Kirby's out there somewhere. Wait till I tell you to go."

ALAN CAILLOU

He saw her standing there with her sister in her arms, a little unsteady on her feet, her naked body bruised and bleeding horribly. There was blood from her back on the floor, a puddle, and he wondered how much she had lost, whether she would make it to the other shore. He said, worried, "I need both my arms, Melanie. You'll have to do it"

"Yes. I know that." The line of her mouth was tight with stubborn fury. "I can make it. I can make it all the way to Hell, just so's I can meet with Simon Kirby there."

"As soon as I start firing, you go. Take this and wait for me there," He tossed her his handgun, the P38, the best handgun ever made. "If you see anybody, anybody at all, kill him, and kill him fast."

He ran to the door, took cover on the deck, and fired three quick rounds into the foliage, to the left, straight ahead, and to the right. A bullet smacked into the timbers below him. He saw the flash of the gun, saw the movement of a camouflage uniform, and kept his eyes on it till he saw a head. He put a single round between its eyes, and waited.

He heard the splash as she entered the water, and then a machine gun was firing at where he had been, but he was no longer there. He saw the gunner, high in a mangrove tree a hundred and fifty feet away, put a single round through his throat, and watched him fall, the gun still chattering.

He was at the other end of the boat now, hidden in the scuppers and watching. He saw a woman out there, running fast through the trees with a grenade in each hand, and he shattered her ankle with one round. He saw her fall as he ducked down and waited till the grenades went off and the fragments were clipping their brittle way through the leaves, and then slipped over the side and swam fast to the opposite bank.

He found Melanie crouched under a mass of sedge there, wiping at Sarah's brow with a handful of wet moss, and he said, "Is she going to be all right?"

138

"I don't...I don't know."

"Keep your eyes open, watch all around us, don't watch what I'm doing. If you see anything, anything at all, fire at it, you understand? Even if it only keeps him under cover till I can get a shot in."

She nodded. He stripped off his emergency pack and broke open the sulfanilamide packet, wishing he had more of it, sprinkling it over Sarah's wounds and gently rubbing it into them. At the top of her thigh, on the inside, the tip of the lash had opened up a wound as far as the bone itself, gleaming whitely. When he had finished with her, he turned to Melanie. "Your back first. Keep your eyes skinned."

He rubbed the powder over her, then moved around to the front of her, on his knees, gently applying the healing salve, watching her face, seeing that her eyes never stopped moving around, from side to side. He could hear no alien sound, and he said at last, "There's a chance at least that he's gone. He can't possibly know how many there are of us. All right, you can lie down now, and rest a little while."

She sank to her knees as shock began to set in. He took off his camouflage jacket and gave it to her. Then he stripped himself bare to the waist, handed her the shirt, and said, "Slip this over Sarah too."

She was beginning to tremble violently now. He put a hand on her and said, "It will all be over, very soon now. But we have a long way to walk. Well, not too far, perhaps..."

She nodded; her voice was hoarse with pain. "I want to go now. I want to get away from this place."

"All right" He bent down, lifted Sarah carefully, and slung her over his shoulder, a slight and easy weight. Letting the Carlson dangle lightly in his right hand, he signaled to Melanie to follow him along the bank of the stream, moving in silence from cover to cover. "Keep the gun ready all the time we're on this side of the water," he whispered. "On the other side, you may run into one of our own patrols, so...You've got eight rounds in the clip, and a good range is up to seventy-five yards. You know about double action hammers?"

She shook her head. He showed her and said; "Keep the hammer cocked—then it's just a touch on the trigger."

Like hunted animals, they crawled through the swamp. When they crossed the weir, Bramble rose up out of the shrubbery and said; "Well, so it's you. I might have known. We heard the firing..."

He looked at the two girls, bloodied half-naked, and said, "My God, is that the family you told me of?"

He had slung his Carlson over his shoulder, and was already taking the frail, limp body of Sarah into his great arms, holding it like a baby, a gentle bear of a man with a look of fatherly anger in his eyes. He said: "The firing...I hope you killed the bastards who did this."

"I killed them. Most of them. Kirby got away, but that's what we always wanted, isn't it? On occasions like these, I wish that weren't so important." He said savagely, "She's a child, a child, and look at her..." He was conscious that the fury was almost out of control. His shirt, hanging loosely on her, was stained with her blood. "What's ahead of us?" he asked.

"Two squads prowling. Captain Duyvel and twenty-six men. This side of the stream is ours now, right back as far as H.Q."

"Good. Get on the sender, tell Rena she's got a couple of casualties coming in. We'll need morphine."

Duyvel came in quietly with Sergeant Hanson. Picking Melanie up bodily, Hanson said, "Hell, you're in no state to walk. Let me help you."

She began to protest. He grinned at her, saying, "My pleasure, Ma'am. If you only knew how long it is since I've had a pretty girl in my arms..." The blood was congealing on her. He held her with infinite care, and the little cortege moved on.

Slowly, imperceptibly, armed men were moving in beside them, silently guarding the flanks as they struggled on.

The hidden headquarters had been enlarged now.

The original crude platform had been strengthened and extended. All of the vast canopy of the mangrove tree was now along and solid room more than thirty feet by fifteen. One wall was hung entirely with the annotated charts, which were covered now with their thin pencil lines in seven different colors. The control console was now in its complete, headquarters form. Its tiny, well-silenced motor was humming so gently that it could barely be heard at all, its light-weight, platinum alkaline batteries replaced every forty-eight hours. Rudi Vicek had taken over the console from Rena, clicking his tongue irritably as he checked it over a trifle annoyed because she had not irreparably damaged it and given him an opportunity to show off his own considerable expertise.

Rena was watching him now, mildly amused by his intensity. "Well?" she said. "You're not going to find anything wrong, you know."

He grunted. "Efrem's on forty-eight point zero one, not zero two."

"There's static coming in on zero one."

"Then you kill it with the jammer. You don't move your frequency."

She was brushing her hair, sorting out the tangles and watching him. "The jammer's busy on the Coast Guard frequency. You want them to lock their directional finders on us?"

He grunted, "Well, you didn't do badly, I suppose, for a beginner."

"Thank you, Rudi." He looked at her and grinned. "I like your hair down—why don't you keep it that way?"

She said, "They leave us alone too much. I don't want to tempt you. That's Bram coming in now."

"I'm not blind." He threw the switch. "Go ahead, Major Bramble."

"We'll be there in three minutes, Rudi," Bramble said. "Drop down the ladder for us, will you? And give me Rena. I'm getting used to her sweet voice on that piano of yours."

"Yes, sir." He passed the mike over to Rena, who said, "Ladder going down, Bram. We're ready for you."

"The two girls, the casualties. I don't want them with us—they need a hospital. And that means questions we don't want to answer. Get hold of Rick and find out what he wants to do. Will you do that for me? Tell him I want a safe hideout, preferably not too far away, the two girls and one man to take care of them—that's all I can spare."

"There's an abandoned cabin on Whitefish Bay. We can fix that up for them. Well out of range of our activities and within easy reach."

"And a doctor? A nurse? They need a lot of care. Maybe surgery."

"I'll talk with Rick."

"Good. Coming in now. Out."

Sarah had at last recovered consciousness. She looked up at Bramble, saw the bristling moustache, the red face, and said weakly, "I can walk, really I can..."

He shook his head. Paul moved in beside them and said, "Here, let me take her now." He cradled her against his bare chest and said, "Just one question, no more. Do they know who we are?"

It was Melanie who answered. "Yes, Paul, they know, I told them...She was very close to tears. I had to..."

"Good. I'm glad. That's the best thing, at this point, that could have happened."

The long rope ladder that had replaced the nylon cord

was there now, ahead of them, seeming to rise up out of the swamp waters and disappear into the mist that constantly hung in mid-air. There was an eerie, ghostly quality to the mist, as though from up there somewhere, out of the clouds, the spirits of the dead would soon be returning to the earth, the spirits of a hundred thousand British, French, and Spanish troops who had died here—was it only two hundred years ago?

For Old Man, a stick of bones and skin now, it had been only yesterday.

And now Rena was crouched over the two girls, patching up their wounds, injecting the morphine, wrapping them carefully like babes in swaddling clothes. The glaze was coming over their eyes. Soon they were asleep.

CHAPTER 12

Coral Gables.

Coordinates: 80.04E
                      25.92N

Flagstaff never knew about the fight on board the houseboat.

He was a strange and silent man, moving around the swamps ever since he had been a young boy, dropping out of the school the Agency had sent him to because there was nothing they could teach him, he thought, that he did not already know.

He had returned to the home he had always loved, where the Cypress Swamp begins to blend in with the Okaloacoochee Slough, and had found, inexplicably, that no one was there. His parents had just disappeared.

For a year he had lived there alone, speaking to no one because no one was there. At last, restless and impatient, he had wandered like an animal in the sedge and the moss, living off the night birds that he killed with his rifle, skinning an alligator or two once in a while and taking the hide in to Immokalee or Miles City to trade for the few supplies he needed, but always returning as fast as he could to the only area where he felt he could survive. An asphalt pavement under his feet was intolerable to him.

And then one day, he had found the family. He had listened to Old Man gravely as the story was told of the Spaniards prowling around, and he had known at once that the old man was quite mad. He had stared solemnly at the two girls, who stared back at him in unabashed fascination, and had decided that this was where he would spend the rest of his life.

Even with Old Man, whom he dearly loved, he would never talk unless it became absolutely necessary. He would listen to what he was told, shake or nod his head, and go off into the swamps to shoot an alligator and bring it back to be skinned. Sometimes he would cook the family's food, always eating, in silence, with them. Sometimes he would just sit on the bank by the broken-down old houseboat and stare out into space, his thoughts hidden away and kept to himself.

Once he went off for two days, to come back with a hammer, a wrench, a box of nails, and some bolts. He spent the next three months repairing the boat—it had been about to fall apart at the seams. This was his home now, and the only place he ever wanted to be.

He had taken Melanie at the end of his first year with them, pulling her down under the bushes and making urgent, surprisingly gentle, and silent love with her. A year later, he had taken Sarah too. And neither of them knew his secret thoughts about them. He would sometimes come to the edge of the bank where the gangplank was and just stand there till one of them, either one of them, would come to him. And then he would lead her away into the swamp and lie with her for half an hour or so, delicately caressing the soft flesh, staring up into the branches when he was finished.

A child had been born once, to Melanie. After a few days it had died, and Flagstaff had crept away in the darkness and cried his heart out. But still he said nothing; he felt that there was nothing that ever needed to be said.

He was a handsome man, strong and stalwart, with an

easy, feline grace to his movements; and the two girls would never know how much he loved them.

He sat now, uncomfortably, in Strickland's office, his brown, scarred feet dressed in unaccustomed slippers, his jeans torn and his tartan shirt ragged. The Captain said, "You don't like to talk too much, do you?"

Flagstaff shook his head, and Strickland continued, "All right, there's a thing called a Private Army in the swamps, and I find that just a trifle hard to believe. Where did they come from?"

Another headshake.

Strickland said, "Colonel Tobin's Private Army. Who the hell is this Colonel Tobin? I never heard of him either. You're going to have to start liking the sound of your own voice, Flagstaff. It's the old boathouse at Frogleg Creek—is that the one?"

Flagstaff nodded.

"And the others? The man named Kirby?"

The Indian said nothing. Strickland sighed and said, "Hell, Flagstaff, you can talk. You wouldn't have come here, all the way here, if you didn't want to talk. So tell me, for Chrissake, who's this Colonel Tobin?"

Flagstaff finally found his voice. "Paul Tobin, a Major. Rick Meyers, a Captain. Many more men. Women too."

"Hell, they've got to be part of Kirby's outfit, this thing they call the CAAA."

He didn't believe it. There was a glimmer, no more, of a light there somewhere, if only he could identify it. He leaned back in his chair and lit a cigar. He stared at Flagstaff and worried about him, and he said at last, "All right, how about going back there and finding out a little more, and reporting back here to me? How about that? There's money in it, if you can use money. These days, who can't?"

The Indian was shaking his head. He got up and said, "I

go now."

The Captain let him get as far as the door and then said gently, "Wait, my friend. There's something I think you might want to know."

The Seminole was standing there, waiting, his face set, one hand at the door. Strickland pulled a sheet of paper from the file on his desk and said, "The old man is dead—did you know that?"

There was no change of expression on Flagstaff's face; he did not move, and Strickland continued, "Someone took his body and laid it out on the road—you know the track that leads to the highway? Laid him out with his hands crossed on his chest, a flower, so help me, in his old hands, a blanket over him. He'd been tortured. Now who would want to crack his skull open with a cord and then lay him out with a flower in his hand?"

Now Flagstaff moved. He went back, sat down slowly, looked at the Captain, and waited.

Nobody spoke.

"How do you know this?" Flagstaff finally asked.

Strickland took a long, deep breath. "What the hell does it matter how I know?"

He held up the paper again, and said, his eyes probing, "We get reports. You know a place called Devil's Garden? Right out there in the middle of the Slough—you know it?"

Flagstaff nodded. There was nothing in the swamp he did not know, and Strickland went on heavily, "We got a call—we get lots of calls. Somebody, *somebody* calls us and says, they're going to hijack a Pan Am plane, they're going to blow up the new bridge, they're going to fire-bomb...*Somebody*. Well, I guess if I knew I wouldn't tell you, but..." He was on the sidelines now, waiting and watching a game that he did not understand, knowing that mischief was afoot in his territory, chafing under the reins that they had put on him; and he was ready to take the bit in his mouth.

He said: "Seems like the old man was born and raised in Devil's Garden; seems he once had a wife there who died when a son was born; the pair of them are buried there. Hell, I've been thirty years at this desk and I never even knew that. They tell me that all he ever wanted was to be buried there too, and it seems like *someone* is too busy to take care of that little chore himself...A note on the body, neatly handwritten, kind of fancy language, a city man's language...Would we kindly take care of this, see that the old man gets his last wish...And I wonder who cracked his skull open like that, and why? And are you sure you don't want to work for me?"

For a moment, Flagstaff just sat there. His face was a shade lighter, almost pale; his mouth was set tight, and there was a burning, furious anger in his eyes. He stood up suddenly and went to the door. The Captain said sharply, "Wait!"

Flagstaff turned. Strickland said, "Just tell me why you came to talk to me, Flagstaff. Will you tell me that, at least?"

The Indian said heavily, "The man Tobin, the other man, Meyers, they made love with my girls, with both of them. It doesn't matter anymore."

He was gone.

Strickland got on the phone to Arthur Reddies. "Art? This time, we're going to make it stick. No one tells me a goddamn thing. By God...they've got a goddamn army of some sort down there in the swamp, a Private Army, and that's my territory. I don't know who the hell they are, the State, the Pentagon, hell, I don't care if it's the White House...I want for you to mobilize the Unit, reactivate it, get it off its communal ass. We're going in there to winkle them out, both the CAAA and this goddamn Private Army...You do like I say, Arthur, and do it fast."

He slammed down the phone and relit his cigar. He was thinking, *They're going to have my badge, that's for sure. But by God, it's going to be worth it.*

* * *

Major Bramble poured himself a long, long drink of Irish whiskey and gestured with the bottle at Rick Meyers. Rick nodded, and Bramble poured another, slapped the cork back into place, and said, checking his watch, "He'll be coming on the air any minute now." He knew he was getting impatient; it was that stage of the operation.

Rick sipped his drink, feeling its warmth in his throat, savoring it, enjoying it fully, holding it up to the light and examining its rich amber color. He said, "I'm worried about Carolyne Southby. I believe she's beginning to think she was tricked, though she doesn't yet know why or how."

"She ought to be told Harry Dewitt's still alive. Though the way he's operating, that happy state might not exist for much longer."

"That's an emotional assessment, Bram. She's suspicious, but she's not sure. That's the way I want her to stay, till this is all over. Then...maybe her father can pull a few strings, have her share a cell with her Harry for the rest of their lives. Her father's a very important man—did you know that?"

Bramble said slowly, "Important to everyone except her. It's sad. The sickness of the generation."

"You're blustering again, Bram. They overtook us and passed us by. Your good health."

They shared the spacious H.Q. together, with no one there but the ever present Rudi Vicek, sitting at his console and watching the dials. It was silent now, the varicolored lights glowing brightly. The twin blue flashed off and on again, and he said quickly, "Major Tobin, Bram."

Bram nodded and took the mike. "Come in, Paul. How does it look?"

"It looks fine," Tobin replied. "Sarah, Melanie, Carolyne Southby, they're all under sedation. The doctor's with them— two nurses to help out. They've agreed to stay there as long as necessary. At the price we're paying them, I suspect they hope it's going to be a long, long time."

"Can you talk?"

"Sure. I'm half a mile from the cabin, out in the swamp."

"What about Carolyne Southby?"

Paul did not sound in the least worried about her. He said, "Well, she's very leery of what's going on, but she's in and out of a semi-coma most of the time. That's the way the doctor's keeping her. If she does decide to run, she won't get very far. I've got Alaric in the house with them, and Serge prowling around outside. I didn't think one man was enough."

"And the two girls?"

His voice was harsh. "Sarah's in a very bad way, I'm afraid. She'll recover, but...Melanie's stronger, seems to be taking even this in her stride. She lost more blood than a stuck pig, but she's...They're a tough breed, Bram."

"The cabin?"

"It's great. Alaric has fixed it up, the stores are in, it looks like a house again. They'll manage very nicely there, What about Rena?"

Bramble still didn't like it too much. "Rena should be in position any minute now. We had her last transmission an hour ago, and I don't expect to hear from her anymore till she's in among them. I'm waiting for a report from Cass. It terrifies me, Paul."

"Yes, me too, a little. It's all up to Cass, isn't it? We have to remember, thank God, that if anything is going to happen to her, we'll get enough warning. We can get her out, even if it means screwing up the whole operation."

"I hope you're right."

"Kirby?"

"He's in Stronghold Eleven, with about eighty men. We're monitoring his radio now. He's got to have more than three or four hundred men along his thin red line. It's not so thin anymore. And a lot of women too, that raises a bit of a problem."

"A problem?"

"Yes. They're just as deadly as the men, perhaps even more so, and still...I've given out the order—the women are to be wounded, not killed, wherever that's possible. It's all we can do, Paul. They're killers, all of them, vicious, mindless killers. They have to expect to end up like this."

"You're pontificating, Bram."

Bramble harrumphed. "Well, it's what I think we should do. Hold on, Cass coming in."

The lights were flashing, and Bramble said to Vicek, "Put the Major on this too, Rudi." He threw the switch and said, "Cass?" His heart was beating fast.

Cass Fragonard said carefully, "So far, so good, Major. She's on her own now, still within my sight."

"A big load on your shoulders, Cass."

"I know. I will take care of her."

"Out, then." He threw the switch again and said to Paul, "You got that?"

"I got it. Have you checked with the Colonel?"

"He's on his way here, should be in very soon. The personal plane and a parachute." He's bringing Pamela Charles and Betty de Haas for a last look at the maps." He grunted. "The one woman in the world I'd allow to check over my charts for me. You'd better get back here fast, Paul. We'll be ready to go very soon now."

"Duyvel is in position?"

"Yes, he is. I told you, we're almost ready to go."

"So I'll be back in four hours. I'm on my way over. Enjoy your Irish, Bram, Out."

The lights went off and on again, steady now, and there was silence. Bram looked at his whiskey and said plaintively, "How did he know?"

Rick threw back his head and laughed. It always pleased

him to see this great, clumsy ox of a man discomforted; he loved him dearly. He said, "Pour me another, Bram, there's a good fellow."

The Major sighed and reached for the bottle. He said suddenly, surprised by his own unexpected thought, "You know, Rick? I've put away more of this stuff in my life than any ten men you can think of. Except for the Colonel himself, of course. And I've never known what it's like to be drunk. How does it feel? Being canned, I mean?"

Rick said: "Don't ever try it...There was a time once, just once..."

He fell into reverie, remembering. It was the waiting period, the time when everything was ready and there was nothing to do but wait for the clock to move on. It was the time to relax and to rest—and neither of them could ever do it.

It was also the time of maximum tension.

Flagstaff had gone back to the houseboat. He approached it in silence; running fast on powerful legs. He had run all the way, and the pain in his lungs was appalling.

He scorned to take any precautions at all. He ran aboard fast, the gangplank hardly shaking under his feet, and his rifle was ready.

He stopped short at the cabin door and then prowled around it, checking the cupboards, the pantry, the little kitchen, and the storerooms. Then he came back, crouched on the cabin floor, and fingered the congealing blood there, smelling the tips of his fingers...

He went back to the shore, checked the heavy footprints in the mud, picked up a few empty shellcases and studied them, and found the bodies of the machine gunners and the snipers lying in the undergrowth, the insects working on them. He found footprints and followed them, the tracks of men in rope-soled boots, two of them carrying burdens, both of which were the women...

He swam across the stream and found the place where there was more blood and the remnants of a yellow powder he could not identify. Then he went back to follow the tracks on the other bank till he lost them in the water. He searched for two hours, till the sun was low, and could not pick them up again. He knew that here was someone who knew about trackers and was leaving no evidence behind.

He returned to the boat, picked up the two torn and bloody shifts of his girls, clutched them to his breast, sank down on the bed, and cried his heart out.

CHAPTER 13

The Swamp.

Coordinates: 81.19E
                    26.15N

They picked her up in the swamp, a lot earlier than she expected.

It was less than two hours since Cass had let her loose, leaving her, apparently, to her own devices in the swirling gray fog that was like a shroud hanging from the gaunt trees, but staying always within both sight and sound of her, hiding himself under the shrubbery, up to his nose at times in muddy water, moving only when she moved.

He saw them long before she did. They were following her too—three Japanese men and a youngish Japanese woman—and he trailed them all, the bait and the hunters, till at last...

She was ready for them, but it was still frightening.

Now it was too late to back out. One of the men stepped forward, his rifle ready, and he was smiling at her. She saw the others moving behind him in the heavy mist. He said, quite politely, "Please, you stay where you are."

He circled round her once, took the bag from her shoulder, and said, "Now you tell me who you are."

She took a deep breath, "My name is Rena Susac." She

was looking at the cotton drab uniform, hoping—a last chance—that they were not what she knew them to be. He said, still smiling, but there was no humor in the smile, "Sit down, please. Sit on the grass over there."

She obeyed him and he turned the bag out and went through its contents carefully. There were two pairs of panties, clean, and a soiled pair wrapped in a plastic bag, a piece of plastic-wrapped soap, a hairbrush and comb, some foot powder, a spare sweater of thin cotton and two tank tops, three Hershey bars and some shelled walnuts, a set of keys on a ring, a small mirror in chrome frame, two ballpoint pens, a small box of junior sized Tampax and a box of pills, half a dozen elastic bands and some bobby-pins, a switchblade knife, a German Walther 9mm automatic pistol, the famous P38 with a spare clip of bullets. There was a cutting from a Miami newspaper with her photograph in it, and another cutting from a European newspaper, written in a foreign language.

He had slipped the pistol almost nonchalantly into his belt, it was the newspaper cutting that intrigued him more than anything. He read it very slowly and hesitantly, as though he were not too fluent in the language. He whistled once, and the Japanese girl came running forward and squatted on her haunches beside him, reading the paper he handed her. They whispered together in Japanese for a while, and the man said at last, "Why you carry this around with you?"

She shrugged. The initial fear was wearing off; there would be more to come. She said; "Just to remind me who I am."

He studied the paper again, questioning his companion when he came across a word that perhaps he did not understand clearly.

It read, in part:

"...and the police are searching for a young woman named Rena Susac, believed to be from Yugoslavia, in

155

connection with the bomb explosion in which three people were killed and $38,000 worth of damage done. The courthouse was a shambles, and the time estimated for its complete rebuilding is seven months. A spokesman has stated that the explosive was a mixture of liquid oxygen and carbon black, known as an L.O.X. or Liquid Oxygen explosive, with the apparent addition of picric acid. This Sprengel-type explosive, the spokesman added, is not in general use in this country, but is popular in parts of Europe, notably in Yugoslavia. The suspect, Miss Susac, is thought to be a Serb. She is believed to be still in the Miami Beach area..."

He stared at the other cutting for a while, the strange and exotic language, held it out to her, and said, "What does it say?"

She shrugged. "The same kind of crap. Just different circumstances, that's all, a different country."

"What country?"

"Yugoslavia. I'm Serbian."

He took up the Miami paper again. Her photograph had as its title, *"Rena Susac: bomber?"* He put it down and began to examine, very carefully indeed, all the other contents of her bag. The two ballpoints seemed to interest him most of all. He broke one of them in two, the ink staining his fingers, and delicately weighed the other with a light touch of his hand, tossing it up and down, wondering about it, writing a few squiggles with it, and finally grunting his satisfaction. He unscrewed the top of the foot-powder bottle and rooted around in it with a stick. He broke the soap into four pieces and wrapped them up again carefully when he was through.

He was thinking hard, the little Japanese, and the two others came forward now and argued interminably in their own language. She waited there patiently for a while, and then said, "If you are who I think you are, you may as well take me to Simon Kirby. He's the man I'm looking for."

156

All their black eyes were on her. The Japanese girl said, her voice a gentle lilt, "What do you know about Simon Kirby?"

She shrugged again, offhandedly. "Nothing. A girl named Carolyne Southby sent me to find him." The first of the men stood up and gestured to her, "Pick up the bag. You come with us."

One of the men who went running off, alone—to take the news where she wanted it to be, she thought. They waited awhile, whispering together earnestly. The Japanese girl was standing apart, watching the captive suspiciously, and Rena was thinking, *The female of the species is more deadly*...She was plump and bowlegged, a peasant woman, with a flat, sallow face, a broad nose, and small, slanted eyes. Her hands were thick and strong, and she could not have been much more than eighteen years old.

The man signaled at last, and she went with them. When they finally reached the hideout, after a long and wearisome journey, Kirby was there, frowning at her, taking the newspaper cuttings from them and studying them intently. "Where did you see Carolyne Southby? Where is she?" he demanded.

"She's dead," Rena replied.

He stared at her, his dark eyes hard. "Dead? How? And how do you know?"

"How do I know? I saw her die, that's how."

For a long time; Kirby held her look. Then he too went through her bag. He took the pistol from the Japanese and emptied the cartridges from it; two bullets had been fired, not recently, "You always reload your gun when you fire it, even one bullet," he growled. "It could mean your life.. What happened to Carolyne?"

"The pigs picked her up and killed her."

He stared at her, very hard.

"Where was this?"

"A place called Pennsuco, on Highway 27."

ALAN CAILLOU

"And that's where you just happened to be, collecting mud for souvenirs."

His dark, angry eyes seemed to bore into her. She said, very offhandedly, "No, what the hell would I be doing in a place like Pennsuco? But that's where she was, and I got the story from her. They picked her up there, some dumb cop or other, but she had a gun on her, shot him and got away. She got to her car and took off and some other cops came running and opened up on her. They put two bullets in her, one in the leg, just a scratch, and the other in the gut. But she made it to Coral Gables. *That's* where I just happened to be, because that's where I live. Don't ask me what she wanted, I don't know. I guess she just wanted a place to lie down and die in, because that's what she did. What was I supposed to do, call in a doctor? She had a hole in her belly you could drive a truck through."

"In that state, she could drive a car?"

"It probably gave her a headache."

Rick Meyers had said, coaching her, "Don't make it sound too plausible, too cut-and-dried. That's always the danger. Remember that few people ever report anything accurately. You must keep the story loose, even unbelievable. If it's too pat, you're in trouble."

"It took her four hours to die," Rena continued, "but there was nothing I could do. And she told me, 'Find Simon Kirby, in the swamp, near Jones Old Town. Just hang around there for a while and he'll find you. Tell him what happened.' So that's what I'm doing. And now, I'd like to get the hell out of this dump."

"You stay."

Rena said calmly, "There's nothing to keep me here."

He grunted: "So Carolyne's dead." It explained a lot, but he still wasn't satisfied: "How come you know her so well?"

"I met her when I came over from Serbia, three years ago. I ran across her in Coral Gables a few weeks back, took her

158

around to the pad I've got there." She corrected herself. "The pad I *used* to have, no good to me now, a dead body in it—unless they found her. Maybe they did, at that. I don't know."

"What's this Serbian paper say?"

"It says the cops over there are still looking for me, but maybe I've gone to America." He didn't like the tone of her voice at all, and he said, "And how come you, carry this sort of stuff around with you?"

"For my scrapbook. Does that make you happy?"

He leaned forward and struck her across the face. "Don't talk to me like that, I don't like it. Where is it you want to go? Back to Coral Gables?"

"No. Just...wander around, the way I always do."

"Blowing things up?"

"Yes, Shake up the middle class democracy a bit, cut the Establishment down to size."

"I'm doing a better job of it. Stay with me and make yourself useful."

"No. Why should I"

"Because you're on the run, and I can use you." He waved the cutting at her and said, "Picric acid in a Sprengel-explosive? That's pretty sophisticated. Where did you learn about that? It's not easy to do."

"Back home, I used to blow a few things up once in a while."

"Make your own bombs?"

"Of course."

"Sprengel, always?"

"No. TNT, most of the time. I know about explosives."

"What's TNT stand for?"

She snorted, and said promptly: "Trinitrotoluene. Trinitrophenol is picric acid, and Cyclonite is cyclotrimethylenetrinitramine, does that convince you? You want to know about PETN? That's pentaerythritoltetranitrate, and if you want any more, I can rattle off a dozen of them. I told you, I'm an expert. Better than Carolyne ever was, and she was pretty damn good too."

"How come she never talked to me about you, never brought you to see me?"

"I told her I was particular who I ran around with."

She thought he was going to hit her again, but he grinned suddenly. "Yes, she wouldn't have told me a thing like that, I'd have sent her to beat up on you. All right, how do you like our American way of life?"

"It stinks."

"Then help me change it. We run with a good crowd here, your kind of people."

"Well..." She hesitated. "Maybe it's not a bad idea at that."

"Surrounded by your peers, all that crap."

A thin, middle-aged man with a bandage round his head had moved in, silently watching, listening. There was blood on the bandage, and his left arm was stiff. He took the piece of paper that Simon Kirby gave him, read it carefully, and said in Serbian, "If this is true, you're quite a girl."

She answered in her own language. "They exaggerate. But yes, I'm pretty good."

"A military aircraft—that's hard to hit with a hand grenade."

"When it's American, it makes it a little easier."

He nodded, read through the cutting again, and said to Kirby, switching back to his easy, faultless English, "She seems to be what she says she is, Major. She can be very useful. Another Serb—we're the best revolutionaries in the world."

There was one more question. "Where did you get that fancy British accent?" Kirby asked.

She said sarcastically, "In Belgrade. They teach us proper English there. You want them to teach us American?"

He nodded slowly. "So let's just be sure, shall we?" He turned to the Japanese and said, "Search her. Everything."

Now she began to shudder. One of the men and the woman between them pulled off all her clothes. She stood there naked while they went through them carefully, feeling in the seams of the blue jeans, studying the buttons of the shirt...Kirby himself went through her bag, and he too paid particular attention to the ballpoint, tossing it back in the bag once more when he was convinced of its innocence. He looked at her and said to the Japanese woman, "Personal search, Mara." The girl came over and said to her, "Bend down." She felt the hard fingers probing, and when she straightened up the woman said, "Nothing, she not hiding anything."

She was glad Cass was out there waiting with it, glad she hadn't brought it with her. She almost had, saying insistently, "Cass, I can hide it..." But he had shaken his head. "You can't even hide a pin if they really want to find it. No, the first time you go to the can, that's where I'll be. You won't have to look for me. They might be watching you, so do just that—go to the can, don't speak, don't say a word. I'll get it to you..."

Soon they were through. They tossed her clothes back to her and let her dress again. All the time Simon Kirby and some of the others gathered around had not taken their eyes off her.

Kirby said, muttering, "Carolyne...What did she tell you about me?"

"Before? Nothing, I never even heard your name, just an idea."

"And after?"

"Before she died? She told me you had raped her. She didn't seem to think it mattered very much, one way or the other."

He watched her buttoning up the shirt, and she said clearly, "But don't try that with me, Major Kirby. I'm tougher than she is, a hell of a lot tougher."

He laughed suddenly. "We'll see about that."

He turned on his heel and disappeared inside. He stuck his head out again almost immediately, and said, "You stay with Milos here, till I get around to finding out how good you really are."

And it was not until nearly two hours later that she found the chance to get away. She was one of *them*, now, mixing easily in with the other Serbs, chatting about the old days in the old country, drinking the strong black coffee they made and prophesying the downfall of their enemies—the old Serbian way of passing the time.

At last she said, grimacing, "For God's sake, where's the can?"

One of them laughed. "A can? There's a hundred thousand hectares of swamp, and she wants a toilet." He gestured. "Our there, Rena, any place you like."

She set down her heavy china mug and walked steadily out into the swamp. She spotted the sentries in the trees, three of them, went a little further, lowered her jeans, and squatted on the ground. In a little while (getting anxious now because she had seen nothing, nothing at all) she heard Cass's voice, a whisper, a zephyr, "To your right side when you get up."

There was no other sound. She stood up, pulled up her pants, scraped mud over the excreta, and found the ballpoint pen, just like her own, lying there to her right. She flicked her own away, picked up the one Cass had left for her, and went on back to the stronghold.

No one paid her any attention at all.

Only Kirby, from his seat at the table, threw her a glance from time to time, assessing her worth. The ballpoint, stuck in the pocket of her shirt, was picking up every word that was spoken, every sound, and relaying it to Rudi Vicek at his console.

She found a sheet of paper and started drawing on it with

the ballpoint. When one of them asked her what it was, she told him, "It's a design for a new kind of land mine I've been working on. Simple enough to make, really, ordinary blasting gelatin, it detonates at 8,000 m. per second..."

They all thought she was fascinating.

CHAPTER 14

Stronghold Eleven.

Coordinates: 81.27E
               26.16N

Simon Kirby, for almost the first time in his violent career, could not understand the Intelligence that had come to him.

He could not measure its meaning, and therefore he could not assess its value. And he was very angry about it.

Stronghold Eleven was the toughest of his line of redoubts, the long line he had placed in apparently haphazard order, but with such close concern for the strategy he had learned in the jungles of Southeast Asia. He knew, had always known, that sooner or later some official body would penetrate the swamp and try and blast him out of there. He had no idea who it might be—the State, or the semisecret force that Strickland had been given to handle, or the National Guard...

It did not matter much to him, either; he knew that from his hidden strongholds he could deploy his men and beat the hell out of any invader. And Eleven was his own, personal hideout.

It lay deep in the Cypress Swamp; close to the undefinable border between Collier and the Seminole Indian Reservation, in an area as lonely and terrifying as a man could imagine. The swamp here was bottomless, mile after mile of stagnant quagmire, from which came up, on the constant mist, the strong sulphuric stench of rotting humus that has lain there for eons.

It was built, as were all the others, of massive slabs of timber. These had been brought in by canoe and dugout and motorboat. He was thinking now of those early days, when the men were beginning to gather around him, when the long-range plans had first been made, when the swamp had been a strange and hostile place.

No more. The old man had, guided him, leading him along the unseen paths, tracking through the streams that wound their ways unexpectedly through the mud, searching out firm ground that was protected by bog on all sides, mapping out the routes of possible entry, plotting the bogs and the streams, and charting the territory so firmly in his mind that now he was as much at home in it as ever the family was.

In those days, he had marveled at the way Old Man had moved, from one stagnant quagmire to another, hobbling through the reaching mangrove roots, staring at one patch of mud that seemed just like the last and saying, with absolute surety, "No, there ain't no bottom to that one..." Or, "The stream here goes underground a mite, about a mile. You got to porter them canoes across here. Watch out for that yaller vine there. It's a bad one, like to make you sick..."

And now Old Man was dead, his treachery punished, a victim of the great God discipline. No matter—he was no longer needed.

Here the ground had been deeply excavated. The stronghold was sunk into the pit, a lean-to more than sixty feet long and thirty wide, covered over with logs and canvas and shrubbery, interspersed with the trailing vine that sought out the empty spaces and flourished there. There were old-fashioned portholes in the walls, covered over with tarpaulins and moss, though he had never intended to hold the refuge in case of attack. It was too vulnerable to the explosives which he understood so well. The stronghold was a resting place, a barracks, a supply depot, no more.

It was a place of absolute security for his men after their operations on the mainland, and the swamp was the barrier that kept the mainland at bay—that, and its perfect concealment.

There were seventy-eight men and women here now, squatting on their heels against the low walls under the sloping roof, cleaning their weapons, gating out of chipped plates which the women brought from the kitchen at the end of the building, or washing their clothes in tin basins, searching out the crawling insects that infested them. One man was getting a haircut, cropping it short and laughing about it.

"The goddamn lice," he said

Kirby was seated at the long plank table, a mug of steaming coffee beside him, his Lieutenants grouped around him. There was Harry Dewitt, just back from Washington, sullen and bitter because his attempt to smuggle twenty pounds of TNT into the Pentagon had failed. He was deeply upset, too, about Carolyne, half convinced that for reasons of his own, Simon Kirby had himself engineered her death. It was a suspicion for which he could not properly account, but it gnawed at the back of his mind incessantly, festering there. He had seen the way Kirby used to look at her, reaching out to touch her once in a while with a nonchalant, proprietary gesture that he hated. Now he was taking the report of her killing all too casually, brushing it aside as a matter of no importance.

His eyes were pale and hostile, his mouth set in a tightly drawn line. He looked across at the skinny, red-headed girl by the stove, and hated her too.

There was Nick Forester, a sniper *par excellence* who was a specialist in the art of cutting down firemen as they fought the fires the others had set. And Joe Satata, a Japanese who had been an exchange student at Stanford three years ago. He was one of the men, in Japan, who had laid the groundwork with the Black September group for the massacre at Lod Airport. He was quiet and studious, and thoughtful—and quite deadly.

There was a slight, muscular black man, with a thick, drooping moustache and a huge Afro haircut, who called himself Allah and who came from Boston. He had stripped to the waist while his woman, one of the young Japanese, washed his swamp-soiled clothes. Allah had spent a long time in Algeria and had been deported when he adopted, and refused to give up, the holy name, though he firmly believed that the CIA had engineered his troubles there with the government. He had once machine-gunned to death a taxi-load of sailors returning at night to their ship in Bizerte, Tunisia.

And finally, there were the two Libyan brothers, Hassan and Abdullah Sallah, who were part of the Command merely because their government had provided Simon Kirby with a token half-million dollars for the purchase, from Russia, of their favorite Kalashnikov weapons, which were fast becoming the most popular revolutionary arms of all time.

And there was one woman, a large-breasted, blonde girl of twenty-eight named Peggy Lepage, who had taken over from Carolyne Southby as his secretary and personal assistant. She had been with the CAAA for less than four months. She had come from San Francisco, where she was wanted on charges of arson, bank robbery, kidnapping, and murder. She had moved into Carolyne's place and into Simon Kirby's bed with an indifferent ease that gave him a deep, sardonic satisfaction.

She sat next to Kirby, her uniform blouse open down to the waist because he liked to look at her from time to time, her long hair falling forward and half hiding the full, tanned breasts, her notebooks in front of her, her pencil poised. It was one of Carolyne's notebooks.

Simon Kirby looked around at the others and drained his

coffee cup. "All right, let's have some attention," he said. "Looks to me like it's going to break any minute now. We better be ready for it. Let's go over the points one by one. First, Strickland gets pulled out, as we all know. We all know too that he was no damn good and was getting nowhere, fast. But since then...Since then, everything we do has turned sour on us. Someone tipped off the pigs about the airline hijack and about the bridge—one of our best days shot to hell. Someone turns the old man and his family against us, and although they never knew very much, it's a bad thing. Someone blew the hell out of our flanking redoubt, which was the best-hidden of all of them—and how did they even find it?"

He swore and said furiously, "Goddammit, that was the one I counted on the most. Ten feet away from it and you couldn't see a goddamn thing, and yet *somebody* found it. Forty-two men dead and half our ammunition supplies blown up."

He turned to Satata. "Joe, you better get twenty, thirty of your men over there as soon as I give the word. I want that position strong again. Spread them out in a line to cover our flank, the usual warning system."

Satata nodded, and Kirby went on: "*Somebody* broke up a little party I had going on board the old man's houseboat and knocked off three of my men. And believe me, they weren't just cops. There was too much expertise going on. They picked up Carolyne Southby and killed her—and how did they know where she was? Can anyone tell me that? I'll tell you how—somebody tipped them off."

He slammed a fist on the table. "Somebody! That's a word I don't like to use! If someone's bugging the hell out of me, I want to know who it is!"

They were uncomfortable with him now, unaccustomed to his uncertainties; Kirby was the kind of man who always knew where he was going and how to get there.

Nick Forester said, "So it's going against us, Simon. It's

not the first time. We just have to stay on top of it, wait till the tide turns. We've done that before."

"Not like this," Kirby said. "What happened to the hijack? What happened to the bridge? What happened to Operation Exeter? Everything's turning sour on us—the last ten days everything we've tried has failed. That's too long a run to be just bad luck."

Joe Satata had taken off his gold-rimmed glasses and was polishing them methodically. He said quietly, "In my country, Simon, I would take all this as an indication that they were beginning to move against us." He was smiling gently. "When the police stop announcing their successes, it means only one thing—that they are expecting greater successes in the near-future."

Allah said eagerly, "That's it, man. They're coming after us. Okay, that ain't no cause to run scared."

Kirby threw him a look. He said, "Harry?"

Dewitt said, "I agree. *Somebody's* got *something* up his sleeve. All right, we've been expecting it. Do we have any reason to believe it's going to be any tougher this time? I don't think we do. We've had a run of bad luck, that's all."

"Sallah?"

Hassan Sallah said stolidly, "Racist, fascist, imperialist American dogs..."

Satata interrupted and said easily, "Yes, we all know that, Sallah. But the purpose of this meeting is not, surely, to convince ourselves of the enemy's known political characteristics; it is to decide what he intends to do."

Sallah said nothing. Kirby stood up and went to the camp stove to pour himself another cup of coffee. Rena was there, and he held out his mug to her, saying, "Carolyne always filled my mug as soon as it was empty."

She looked at him without emotion. "Tell that to Peggy Lepage. There's a long way to go before you and I reach that

169

stage. You want a sandwich?"

He shook his head and went back to the table. They were beginning to argue among themselves there, the two Libyan brothers spouting the phrases they had been taught, and Forester and Satata ganging up on them.

Kirby said, "Shut up! There's something else. Did anyone ever hear tell of a man named Colonel Tobin? Seems like he runs a Private Army."

There was a puzzled silence.

Nick Forester, frowning, shook his head, and Kirby went on. "That's all I've got, a name. They could be Federal, State, the Pentagon for all I know. Who knows, it might be the CIA playing ass-buggers again, only I think they're too smart for that. But I tell you one thing..." He leaned forward on the table. "I don't give a damn who they are or where they come from. Looks to me like a showdown, and that's what I've been waiting for."

He laughed shortly. "An Army? What do they mean by that? A company? A battalion? A division? Hell, I don't care if it's an Army Corps, we're impregnable in here, and that's exactly what we're going to teach them."

Somebody said, uncertainly, "A Private Army?" and Kirby nodded. He said again, "That's all I've got. The Private Army of Colonel Tobin. I don't know who he is, and I don't know who they are, or where they come from. I only know one thing, and. that is—we beat the hell out of Strickland's men, and when he brought in the Guard we gave them a headache too, and if they've got some burlesque outfit to throw at us now..."

He was furious, recounting his recent losses and smarting under them. "Okay, they want a fight, that's what they're going to get. Only this time, I don't want any leftovers. I want them cut to pieces. I don't want a goddamn survivor to crawl out of this swamp, not a single goddamn man."

He laid a hand on Peggy Lepage's plump thigh, the blue jeans stretched tight, and said, "Take this down, get the orders out. Satata's men to take over the flanking area, right away, hole up there and wait on a line dead north and south one hundred yards west of the wreckage of the redoubt. All other units to move out of their barracks and take the west bank of the stream..."

He looked at Satata and said, "I'm relying on you, Joe. I don't want anyone past your line. The moment you start firing, we move in from the river and take a half circle to the north of you. We'll be two miles out and you can drive them into our guns. Fall back the moment we make contact with them."

He stated his orders clearly, at great length, and Peggy Lepage took them all down on her pad. Rena came closer and watched them, eating a hamburger and not paying very much attention. And when he had finished, at last, he said; "All right, that's it. Any questions?"

Abdullah Sallah said, "My unit needs more grenades. We're down to less than a hundred."

"Pick up all you need at the warehouse; better get on to it right away. Rifle ammunition?"

"We're in good shape."

"There's sixty-five more cases on board the barge. Get someone to check out all units and see what they need. Anything else?"

No one spoke, and Kirby laughed shortly. He said, "We call a break. For the time being, no more anti-American activity. We just sit tight and wait for them to move in on us. And then, we show that goddam Colonel Tobin and his goddamn Private Army the way an army really fights."

He turned to Peggy Lepage. "Rustle me up a couple of cans of beer, for Chrissake. And somebody open a few vents—it smells like a whorehouse in here."

Outside in the darkness, lying motionless under a pile of sedge, oblivious of the leeches that were sucking the blood from his arms (and wondering what they thought about his tin legs),

Cass Fragonard, the tiny plug in his ear, was listening to the voices inside the stronghold.

Eleven miles away, Paul Tobin was listening too. The big console was humming softly, seeming to purr its satisfaction as Rudi Vicek delicately turned the dials that kept the scanner dish properly aimed. He said quietly, "The yellow dot at two o'clock on the dial, it's Cass. Fragonard, he's forty feet away from them."

Paul Tobin nodded. He passed his sheet of shorthand notes to Major Bramble, and said, "There's the enemy battle order, Bram. Now, it's all yours."

The huge private plane, a highly modified 747, was heading for Key West with all its papers in order. The manifest read, "No passengers," and that was how it would land at the airport there.

But now there were three people in the enormous lounge, Colonel Matthew Tobin, his confidante Pamela Charles, without whom he rarely traveled anywhere, and Betty de Haas. Looking at her now; admiring the taut bulges under her jumpsuit, he was thinking, *Betty too, she's good to look at, to touch, to caress, to love...*

The interior of the plane was nearly all lounge. It had been fitted out with thick blue carpeting, leather armchairs in a rich brown, a large writing desk in ornately carved walnut that had once been in the London house of Samuel Pepys, and a beautiful walnut bar along the cockpit's bulkhead.

Moretti was at the controls now, with Jan Wicewski as co-pilot, and Drima, the Maltese, as navigator, with four other members of the Private Army as crew.

It was dropping from its cruising altitude and slowing down, the powerful engines almost silent as it made a four-degree turn and slipped softly down through the clouds, Drima said over the loudspeaker, "Eighteen more minutes, Colonel. Door opens in fifteen."

The sliding door; part of the considerable modifications, had been fitted aft of the great wings on the port side. The Colonel said cheerfully, "Well, we'd better start thinking in terms of parachutes, hadn't we?"

Pamela Charles, her long, slim body in a tightly knit jumpsuit (it was the regulation design and color, but had been made for her by the Marchesa in Rome), had poured them all their final drink of Irish whiskey and was closing up the bar, pushing the button that slid the panels into place.

She slipped the harness over her shoulders and turned her back dutifully so that the Colonel could check it for her. Tightening the straps, he ran his hands over her—slim waist, pronounced hipbone, almost angular, and long slim thighs that were smooth and resilient, breasts that were small and high and astonishingly firm, tightly pointed.

He turned to Betty and helped her too—plumper and always bouncing, with a firm, schoolgirl body that he could never keep his hands off. He checked the static lings carefully and turned for Pamela Charles to check his, feeling the sharp tugs as she went through the drill with practiced ease.

He stood close to the door, waiting for it to open, Pamela Charles next to him and Betty close by. Again he said, "Try to keep close. It's all a bit of a mess down there."

Drima's cheerful young voice came over the speaker, "I've locked in the finder, Colonel. We'll be over the dropping ground in seven minutes."

"Ground wind velocity, Drima?"

"Negligible, Colonel. Humidity's high, conditions are perfect."

The needle of the altimeter was at two thousand, and the great plane was still sliding down. Betty said, trying to keep the excitement from her voice, "There's more than a mile of open space there. We shouldn't have any problems."

He smiled. He knew that she wasn't happy in a parachute and wondered if she had caught the slight phobia from Bram, her other lover; or if he, perhaps, had caught it from her. He squeezed Pamela Charles' arm, and saw the faint smile at her lips.

"Door opening, stand clear please," Drima announced.

The Colonel slewed around in his chair to make sure they had moved back before he pressed the button. The wide door slid silently open, and they felt the rush of wind, heard the sound of the jets. The lights had come on, a long row of them over the opening, six red and one green. He checked his watch—eight-fifteen in the evening, two minutes ahead of schedule. He stared at the lights and waited, then patted both women affectionately, saying, "Remember, as close to me as you can manage, Paul and some of the others will be there, so let's make it nice and tidy for them...Here we go."

Drima shouted, "Go!" and he jumped.

He looked up and saw the two of them silhouetted against the gray sky, listened to the beep-beep-beep of his finder, pulled one of the directional cords to change his angle a trifle, and landed lightly in the night air, pulling in on the lower cords of his chute as it collapsed around him, looking around for the others and seeing Pamela Charles land as lightly as he had, and Betty de Haas falling on her back and rolling over, pulling in furiously as though there were a high wind blowing.

He ran towards her, and Paul was there helping her up. She held out her arms, all covered over with wet mud, and said, "My God, it's disgusting..." The mud was squelching under her feet. Paul laughed and said, "You get used to it."

He shot out his hand. "How are you, Dad? A good trip? That was a nice jump."

"Well, when you've been at it as long as I have...How are you? Everything going as it should?"

"So far, yes. We're in position, and so is the enemy."

"No interference from anyone?"

"No, sir."

"Bramble satisfied with the planning? And Rick?"

"Both of them."

"Good."

Sergeant Roberts was there, with two of his squad—Asa and Yehud—helping them out of the harnesses and rolling up the parachutes. He managed a surreptitious pat at Betty's plump little behind, and she squealed. He said cheerfully, "Nice to have a few more ladies around. We're collecting them."

Colonel Tobin said, "Ah yes, the ladies. How are they?"

"They're installed in a beach house, Alaric and Serge looking after them, a team from the hospital as well. So far, no difficulties."

"I was sorry to hear about that poor old man. Pity you couldn't have got there a little earlier."

Paul said, sadly, "It was purely fortuitous that I got there at all, I just wanted to check with Old Man on a track he'd pointed out, which had disappeared under the mud. When I got there..."

He hated to remember it, thinking about the savage, opened gashes on the girls' bodies. He said, "Nice if I could get Kirby myself. As a matter of fact, there were a couple of times I could have killed him, but...Yes, you were right, of course. He's got them all together for us, and without him, that might never have happened."

"And Strickland?"

"No trouble. No sight or sound of him."

"Good. So let's get moving. I want to see this crow's nest of yours..."

But Strickland was in the swamp.

175

With Arthur Reddies, a fast moving, highly capable executive officer, he had gathered his Unit together, one hundred and thirty men from the Police Department, the National Guard, and the Sheriff's Office, all banded together into the special force that had once had the directive to wipe out the CAAA but had since been placed in a state of suspension.

They all knew, these men, that Strickland had disobeyed his orders. They all knew that his job, and theirs, had been put on the line, but only three of them had refused to go along with him. They too had been impatient, angry at the secret orders that had come, it seemed, from the highest possible authority, even though every move the terrorists made, a pattern, was clearly aimed at putting that authority in the worst of all possible lights. It was not merely antisocial, their activity; it was patently anti-American.

But one of these three had spoken to Washington on the phone, and Arthur J. Wagnall was coldly furious.

There was nothing much he could do; Strickland had gone, with all his men, and was out of further contact. He thought of sending some of his men after him, but decided against it. How would they find him in the great swamp? He had called London at once, and a soft-voiced young girl, very reserved and discreet about it, had told him the Colonel was not available. She would see that he got the message at the earliest opportunity.

He was furious; but the Unit was in the swamp, and the men were eager for action.

They were moving now; with Strickland at their head, due north from Monroe, where the trucks had taken them, plodding through the mud and the slime with their rifles held high and their heavy packs on their backs. Four Seminole Indians, went ahead of them, cutting a path through the dense, stifling vegetation.

Strickland said, "Thirty miles of this goddamn stuff, it's

more than a man can bear..."

His tightly laced rubber boots were already half filled with the black mud, and there was a red gash at his knee where he had fallen. But the sound of the men behind him was a comfort. When he looked back and saw their hard, stern faces, he knew that at last he was settling the score. He thought of his wife, still under the plastic surgeon's care, and he said aloud, "It's not the pain she had to suffer, it's the fright—they scared her stiff..."

Someone behind him said, "Huh? How's that, Captain?" and he grunted. He said again, "Thirty miles, we break soon for a meal, soon as we can find some dry ground."

Reddies had moved in beside him. "You know where we're headed? Or are you just guessing?" he asked mildly.

Strickland said shortly, "We're headed for the one place I think they might be. And if we don't find them there, we head someplace else. And if they're not there, someplace else again."

"Sixty-four hundred square miles of swamp—that's a lot of territory to cover, on foot."

"The last report we had, before they saw fit to replace me with a bunch of amateurs...They were southwest of the ruins of Sam Jones' Old Town. It's my guess they're still there."

"Your guess, or your hope?"

Strickland sighed. "Just a hope, Art. Yes, that's all it is. We may just be jerking off. But I don't aim to sit on my butt any longer."

He pointed to the men behind him. "For God's sake, Art, a hundred and thirty men and they're all with me! How many backed out? Three! That's a pretty good poll about the way we all feel."

"And one of those three called Arthur Wagnall in Washington, did you know that?"

"Yes, I know it. And Arthur J. Wagnall can go and jerk off too." He added wearily, "It's just gotten to be too much, Art.

I should have done this the moment they cut Jane up like that. I don't know why I didn't. Maybe I'm getting old."

He looked at Reddies suspiciously. "You want to pull out? All you have to do is say the word, I won't hold it against you."

Reddies grinned. "The last few days before they put us out to pasture, let's enjoy them."

"You're a good kid, Art. And don't worry about where we're heading. We've got a hundred and thirty men, and they've got—what? Five hundred? Who can be sure? We don't have to find them. They are going to find us. You still with me?"

Reddies nodded. "I'm with you. We all are."

The column forced its way on, through the mud and the spreading roots, through the big cypress clusters and the moss and the vines.

And always, the wet mist swirled about them, half hiding them; it seemed the thirty miles would never come to an end.

CHAPTER 15

The Swamp.

Coordinates: 81.22E
                 26.47N

Ahmed Idriss wished he were back home in the dry and brittle heat of his Sahara Desert dunes; he found the clinging gray mist of the Swamp an affront to his sensibilities.

He was a ghoul, motionless in the bog, crouched on his heels under the roots of the giant trees; and he drew his *jurd*, the Arab cloak he always wore, tighter around him. His voice was very low and careful; in this dank, confining mass of vegetation there was far more danger than in the lonely solitude of his deserts. There, if someone approached, you could see him ten miles away, and the camels would give warning the moment he crossed the horizon. But here...

He wondered if the sheltering foliage sheltered the enemy too.

For an hour, he had personally scouted the area, leaving his men hidden together, and now he was back and saying quietly, "The ears, the ears are more important than the eyes here. We can see little, but we can hear everything. They will be careful, these men, but they cannot move like us, and so...We will hear them if we listen well, Now, my children..."

They were grouped around him, listening.

There were Reddigan and Brennan, the two incorrigibles; Smith, about the best of the long-range bowmen; the Ethiopian Aklilu; Hamash the Turk; and Romulo, who had once been the Argentine's top toxophilite, winner of more cups and shields and ribbons than he could count.

They crouched down on their heels in the mud, all of them emulating their group leader. They listened both to him and to the sounds of the alien swamp, their bows held lightly across their knees, their quivers of cedar shafts over their shoulders.

The bows were handmade, the old-fashioned longbows that were still the best in the world if you knew how to fashion them. Each man, on the Colonel's order (and on Ahmed Idriss' advice), had made his own.

"Your life depends on your bow," the Colonel had said, "and I want to be damn sure you know that if it fails you, it's no good taking it back to the store. It's your own damn fault and you deserve it."

They had been carefully tillered from staves of yew that had matured for a minimum of eight years. These staves were hard to come by nowadays, but there were still stocks of them in the Far East. They had been steam-straightened and sanded patiently to size because neither Idriss nor the Colonel would permit the use of cutting tools; and each one was a work of individual art. Their bowstrings were of Fortisan, which the Colonel grudgingly admitted was better than linen.

With a slight touch of sarcasm Idriss said, "We're expecting a maximum of thirty men, so that means thirty arrows. If we use forty someone's going to have to answer to me for it." He grimaced. "Oh, maybe you won't be able to get a clean shot every time, because of the trees. But once they come into sight, they'll be moving along the edge of the stream, no doubt, and that's' where we hit them."

He looked around at their lined and weathered faces,

knowing they were all experts. "Thirty shafts should be enough—that's five flights apiece—let's not have any nonsense about it. My first shot will be a screamer, and that's your signal. Right to left, each man takes the first five of the enemy, so remember your position numbers."

He said sourly, "We don't want one man with a dozen arrows in him and another six of them running free. Remember, I don't want a single shot fired back at us. I want absolute silence all the way. Any shooting it's going to tell the others that something unpleasant is happening to their flank guards. I don't want that. All right, string your bows."

He stood up and watched them at work. "Reddigan and Brennan right up in this tree, the others—forty feet apart out on the flanks. I'm placing you all myself. We make a half-circle round the old redoubt, just in case they don't use the path by the water. But they will, because they've got to be silent too, and their machetes would make too much noise. Any questions?"

Brennan said, "What time do we get to eat? I'm hungry."

"Go to hell, Brennan." He said again, insisting, "Fast, I want this over fast, before they've time to start firing. I take the last three men in the column myself—that'll be the longest range. Hamash the first five, because he's just a lousy Turk and doesn't know how to use a bow properly, none of them do..."

Hamash said happily, "May I remind you, you Bedouin bastard, that the Turkish records have never been broken? In nearly three hundred years?"

Idriss went on: "Aklilu the second, then Reddigan and Brennan, Romulo, and then Smith. I'll take care of any stragglers, or anyone out of range of you bastards."

Smith said, "Mongolian draw, no one's going to be out of range. I don't care how far away they are."

"They be close enough. Wait for the screamer—that's the signal. Once you're in position, nobody moves, nobody even breathes, or God help you. Let's go."

He jerked a thumb at the top of the tree they were under, and said, "Brennan, Reddigan, up you go. The wreckage of the redoubt is dead behind you, half a mile off."

He crawled through the undergrowth with the others, placing them just where he wanted them. Then he went back to the stream, built himself a shelter of sedge, and crouched behind it, waiting.

And it was four and a quarter hours before they came. In that time, there had been no unaccustomed sound at all, nothing to tell the approaching enemy that seven men, skilled archers, were lying in wait for them, their arrows ready, their muscles strong.

They came, as Idriss had predicted, down the edge of the stream where the going was quieter, and he saw that they were keeping well to the shelter of the shrubbery, close into it. He thought about Hamash and Aklilu, both of them on the foliage side and therefore in difficult positions, and he said to himself, "Well, I'll take care of them if they're not fast enough."

He did not move. His bow was across his knees. He raised it slowly, testing the tension on the string, watching the dull sheen of the hunting head and the green of the stripped base fletching. These fletchings, too, were no longer commercially obtainable, but the Colonels bowmen made their own, from goose feathers, grinding them down by hand.

The men, as Paul had told him, were all Japanese. They were moving easily and lightly, one man well ahead of the others, with another, he saw, well out on the left flank, the other protected by the stream. He stared out across the water for a while, and saw nothing there. A mistake—they should have had a man on the right flank too.

He thought about it for a while and decided that Kirby would not make such a mistake, Idriss knew that out there *somewhere*, hiding himself with unusual care as he moved along, there had to be one more man.

He counted them—thirty-two all told, and perhaps one more across the river.

The head of the column was three hundred yards away now, its tail nearly twice as far. He waited.

The lead man, he saw, was searching the mud for footprints, and he grinned; they had kept to the shallow waters there.

Soon the column was coming within easy range. He reached back and touched the shafts in his quiver, assuring himself that they were in precisely the right position. He took one out slowly, fitted it, drew back the string to his nose and jawbone, and let fly. The screamer head whistled the signal.

Now his movements were fast as lightning, He had four shafts in the air before the first hit home, a strike in the throat of the last man, passing clean through his body and shattering the spinal cord as it went. He saw four men fall, in silence. Then the others were letting loose their arrows too, and he watched the Japanese crumple and fall, sinking down to the silent mud and the water. One man, up front, was running, his rifle ready, searching for a target, and in the one brief instant of time that was the delay. Idriss broke his neck with a fifth shaft.

He heard the angry hiss of the arrows cutting their way through the damp air, heard the sharp clip of them as they went through the leaves, heard the dull thud of them striking home.

And now he saw him—the man on the other bank. He was crouched low, running for cover, not understanding perhaps that men could be killed in silence, so quickly. Idriss pulled back his bowstring once more and sent his shaft cutting deep into the man's chest, under the left armpit and six inches below it. He saw the man spin around with the force of the blow and, to make sure, sent his final arrow into the throat.

He had counted seven seconds. Seven seconds from the time of the screamer to the last flight from his own bow.

He waited. He checked his watch and studied the under

growth carefully. There were no more of them coming up.

And in fifteen minutes exactly, he sent a final screamer hurtling up into the air above him, watching it fall close beside him and gathering it up again, cleaning off the carbon-steel head carefully before going off to the rendezvous at the base of the tree.

Soon they were all together again. "Shaft count, please," Idriss said.

Hamash said, "Six. I got one of Aklilu's for him while he was lighting his pipe."

Aklilu grunted. "Four, I think you got one of mine too, I couldn't get in a clean shot."

"Reddigan?"

"Five."

"Brennan?"

"Five."

The other two, Romulo and Smith, at long range, had each fired six flights, and. Idriss said, "Good, that's the way it's supposed to be. Now go recover your shafts, clean them up, check them for straightness, and we'll be on our way. But I want the bodies under cover, just in case anyone happens to pass this way."

He saw Romulo beginning to unstring his bow and glared at him. The Argentinian champion sighed, slipped the loop back over the notch again, and said, grimacing, "Just a matter of principle, Ahmed..."

Idriss grunted. "You're not finished yet, you wait for the order anyway. An archer with an unstrung bow is like a Bedouin without a camel."

"And," Romulo mocked him, "a man without a wife?"

Idriss sighed. He pushed over the slide on his sender and said quietly, "Come in, Apple. This is Group Charlie."

"Go ahead, Charlie," Bramble answered.

"Objective destroyed, no casualties."

At the other end, out of the treetops now, Major Bramble said with great satisfaction, "Now, he's got no flanking cover. Let's hit him."

Paul Tobin nodded. "Go, Bram. He's all yours."

The Colonel was in contact with London, standing by the big console and glaring angrily at the flashing lights that told him the scramblers were on. He had slipped the mike around his neck and was using the earplug.

"Well, get hold of Mr. Bloody Wagnall again," he said. "And tell him I won't be responsible for Strickland's life, nor for the lives of any of his bloody men. If he gets in my line of fire I'll have his guts for a necktie..." He broke off and said, scowling, "No. Cancel that. Maybe I can turn his damned stupidity to some advantage. Give me that jumping-off place again, Monroe?"

He was checking the map: "I've got it." He threw quick glance at his watch and said, "How long ago? Then he must have covered fifteen miles or so, more if he's moving fast...God damn his eyes...All right, tell Wagnall I'll cope with it."

He nodded to Rudi Vicek, slipped off his mike and earplug, and said, "A hundred and seventy-two degrees, Rudi. Swing your dish around and tell me what's there."

He watched the wire-mesh saucer gyrating. Rudi looked at the pale-green marking on the screen and said, "Another body of men, I'd say about a hundred of them, right behind us. Not too much metal there, probably only rifles."

"Distance?"

"Four miles, Colonel, a trifle over. And they're stationary."

"Can you hold them on auxiliary?"

"Yes, sir. Won't be as clear, but I can track them."

The Colonel sighed. He said, grumbling, "No discipline

in this country. That's Strickland. Get me Paul on closed channel."

Rudi twisted the dials rapidly and pushed the little red button that meant *urgent*. When Paul was on the air the Colonel said, "Strickland's in the swamp, Paul, with about a hundred men. Twelve miles south of you at the moment, your bearing of...Wait a minute."

Rudi said quickly, "A hundred and seventy-nine, Colonel."

"A hundred and seventy-nine. He's not moving at the moment—probably stopped to eat a hotdog or something—but I'm monitoring. I'll let you know when he moves on. You're closing in, I see."

"Yes, sir. And it's time to get Rena out. Will you call Cass direct for me? I want her out in five minutes."

"Will do. Anything else?"

"Nothing."

"Out then. Good luck, Paul."

Rudi closed down the channel, and opened up on Cass Fragonard. The Colonel said, "Rena, Cass. In five minutes. Out."

Cass Fragonard's lightweight legs were heavier than usual. The water of the swamp, mixed with its viscous black mud, had found its way into their intricate maze of steel cables, and it squelched when he moved. He eased himself out of the morass, dragged the covering sedge tighter about his head and shoulders, and slid along the ground to the point he had chosen. He was watching the stronghold carefully, watching, too, the three sentries up in the trees, and he thought, *Easy shots for the first two, but the other man there...*

Very carefully, very silently, he took off both his legs, emptied the mud out of them, hitched them up again, and flexed the metal muscles easily. He looked at his watch. When he was ready, he took out the slingshot and two steel balls, killed the first two sentries with quick, powerful shots to the center of the forehead, watched them both crash to the ground, and waited. He was watching the third man.

He saw him start, saw him staring down at the fallen bodies of his two comrades, saw him take out the whistle and blow a furious blast on it, three times in quick succession.

He pulled himself deeper under the cover of his camouflage and dragged himself inch by inch toward the tree that was their rendezvous. He was thinking happily, "All right, Rena *mon petit chou*, now it's up to you..."

The sentry up in the tree was staring down at where Cass had been, fingering the trigger guard of his Kalashnikov nervously.

Cass took out is slingshot again and killed him.

Simon Kirby was startled.

For a moment, at the sound of the warning whistle, he had frozen. The men had reached quickly for their weapons and were looking at him. He said softly, "So someone has gotten through—that sonofabitch Satata...All right, you all know the drill. Watch out, they're close in on us. Anything moves, kill it."

One of them was already opening the heavy timber exit, dragging aside the cedar slabs and peering through the camouflaging shrubbery out into the swamp. He whispered, "A burst of machine-gun fire out there..."

Kirby shook his head, "No, we get into position first, we're too good a target here if they've got mortars. Hurry it up."

Silently, one by one in careful Indian file, the men began snaking their way through the mud and the overhanging moss, taking up the positions that Kirby had given them for the battle, a long line to the west along the edge of the stream.

They were almost invisible in the heavy mist, dark shadows moving in dark shade, easing silently along through the shrubbery. Cass counted twelve of them, each man ten paces ahead of the man behind him, each man beginning to spread out in competent open order, and then Rena was there, crawling along in her allotted place. He saw her disappear under the bushes and he waited. Soon she was beside him, trembling now with the relief. He put out a hand and held her arm, then grinned at her, a finger to his lips.

Soon all the men had gone, and the stronghold was empty. She whispered, shuddering, still not quite believing it, "Suppose they had decided to stay inside and hold it?"

He shook his head. "We blew up one of his redoubts. He knows they're deathtraps now—I told you." He grinned at her easily, conscious of her shaking. "If he had, we'd have had to replace you, wouldn't we? And where would we find someone else like you?"

Silently they eased their way back to the stream, swimming across it under water. Bramble was there waiting for them.

The Major heaved a deep, deep sigh. He put his arms round Rena and held her in a huge bear hug for a moment.

"My God, I didn't really believe you'd get away with it."

He thumped Cass Fragonard on the back, and Cass said, "They're all out. They've pulled back. What about the others?"

"A man watching each of his redoubts. They're all pulling out. He's got a message through to them all—by runners, presumably. He's keeping radio silence."

Bramble put his sender close to his mouth and said quietly, "She's out, Colonel," and the sound came back through the earplug, "All right, Bram, get her over here. I want her well away from the fighting. I'll pass it on to Paul direct."

"Out."

The Major looked at Cass and beamed. He said, "In thirty-five minutes, we go. Take her home, Cass."

He patted her behind and watched them moving off till the mist and the trees had hidden them from his sight.

CHAPTER 16

The Swamp.

Coordinates: 81.21E
                    26.19N

     And now, the final phase of the battle was beginning. The site had been chosen by the enemy and pinpointed by the Private Army. It was no longer anything more than one kind of force against another.

     The long line of the Private Army, facing the hidden enemy on a five-thousand-yard front, was sparsely stretched out in ones and twos and threes, fifty yards or more separating the groups.

     They were carrying their Carlson guns, digging their foxholes and earthworks, and setting up the deadly 4.2 inch mortars. These mortars would hurl a 24-pound flat-bottomed shell up to 4,500 yards in sixty seconds, and where there were three men to a crew, they could send nine shells spinning through to the target before the first one hit.

     Rudi Vicek had been brought down here now, with the portable auxiliary of his console, the radar scanner, and the VUPR finder. He was cursing to himself as, with two men detached to help him, he lugged the heavy packs from unit to unit, pinpointing the force that was facing him.

ALAN CAILLOU

Major Bramble had said, "The range *ought* to be four hundred yards, but their line won't be exactly where we've estimated it, no doubt, so let's be certain, shall we?"

And so, from point to point, he had lugged the backpacks along with him setting them up and swearing softly.

He said, "Three miles, for God's sake, in this mess, and they want it in two hours. It can't be done..."

Mendoza, grinning at him and digging in his mortar, said cheerfully, "Good for your waistline, Rudi. Just tell me exactly where they were—I'm on this one by myself." His voice was very low.

Rudi whispered, spinning the dial and watching the delicate needle, "Four hundred and seventy-two yards to your dead front center, spreading out to five hundred and twelve on the left flank, down to four hundred and ten on the right. Machine guns only, I'd say, maybe eighteen or twenty of them. You'd better dig in good."

"Angles, Rudi, I need angles."

"Forty degrees right, and a little more to the left—that should do nicely. Who's up ahead of you?"

"Holmes. He's lucky, he's got two Carlsons to back him up."

"See you, Mendoza," Rudi whispered and moved off.

All senders were on open channel, and Bramble was coordinating the positions as the reports came in. He said to Paul, worrying about it, "Now that we've got them all pinpointed, I wonder if they're going to change their line? That'll be nice, won't it?"

Paul shook his head. "Chances are, they're pretty well dug in, that's why I want the mortars. If they had a second line ready, we'd know about it."

Bramble was moving the yellow pins of the chart. When midday came and Rudi had returned to base, the Major said quietly into the sender, "All units, stand by." He looked at Paul,

190

who said, "Well, it's now, or never. Whenever you're ready, Bram."

Bramble said, raising his voice, the time for silence gone now, "All units...Mortars begin firing."

He heard the loud blast of them as all down the line the shells went shrieking into the swamp, so fast that a man could believe they were automatic cannon. He heard a shriek and a scream and a shout from the other side, and the Kalashnikovs were answering their fire, their chatter loud and insistent. The men with the Carlson guns crouched in their foxholes and waited for the barrage to die down. The roar of the guns was incessant, and at the end of seven minutes, Bramble said, "All units, cease your mortar fire."

Now, there was only the rattle of the Kalashnikovs, still heavy but less than before. He waited a minute and said, "Mortars stand by," and in a moment, "Mortars, resume firing."

The din was appalling. It seemed as though the swamp itself were shaking and roaring its anger at them. Suddenly Vicek said, watching his dials, "A big gun, Major, coming in from the right."

Bramble turned. "Show me."

Rudi indicated the sweeping needle of the radar and said, "There, at two o'clock, moving across our front, well back. It's moving fast—there must be a track there."

They watched the green spot on the dial, listened to its gentle ping-ping-ping, and when it stopped moving, Bramble said sharply, "Narrow your dish, fifteen degrees. I want to know what that is."

Rudi swung the balanced knob over quickly and said, "Fifteen degrees." He peered darkly at the green spot. "I make it light artillery, one piece, could be a 75mm field gun. How the hell do they move it around in this morass?"

"Manpower," Bramble said. "All it needs is muscle."

Then, into the sender, "All units, continue firing for three

191

minutes. Edgars Jefferson, can you hear me?"

Jefferson's voice came in loud and clear, "I can hear you, baby."

Bramble repeated patiently, "Can you hear me, Jefferson?" He could hardly hear himself speak, but Jefferson replied, "Yes, sir, Major. I can hear you, Major sir."

"There's a heavy gun standing right opposite you. As soon as the mortars stop, get out there and spike it. Range is...What is it, Rudi?"

He was turning the wheels furiously, scribbling the cross-calculations on his block. "It's moving again, Major, coming in closer, six hundred and forty yards now, moving very slowly."

"Then they're off the track and trying to get it just where we want it to be...About six hundred, Jefferson."

"Would that be feet, Major?"

"Yards, you idiot. You've one minute to go, then get out there and take care of it."

"Yes, sir."

Jefferson waited. In the sudden diminishing of the uproar, he leaped out of his foxhole and raced across the intervening ground, crashing through the shrubbery, swinging his machete with his left hand, his Carlson ready in his right. A swathe of bullets went past him. He threw himself to the ground and yelled, "Gopa! You stupid mother, take care of that machine gun for me!"

He heard Gopa, the Nepalese, yell back, "Then get out of my way, you black bastard!" He wriggled himself deeper into the soft earth, and heard Gopa's Carlson, on rapid three, cutting into the undergrowth ahead of him; the machine gun stopped firing, and a man was moaning. Jefferson got up again and ran on. A bullet sliced through his ear, and he cursed and dropped again. Someone was coming at him with a grenade ready, and Jefferson cut him down with one bullet.

He saw the gun now, a Japanese light artillery piece, the

70mm howitzer they had used, because of its extreme mobility, in the jungles of Southeast Asia. It was three hundred yards away from him, standing in a clearing, and six men were at its wheels, wrestling it along. Its armor plating had been stripped off, and he growled, "Just my luck, no place for impact..."

He began to worm his way around to its front, listening to the sound of the Kalashnikovs, too close to him for comfort now. Did they know he was there, among them?

There was a movement, a sound, high above him. He rolled over onto his back, fired, and saw his target—a machine-gunner—come tumbling out of the tree. He ran on till the howitzer, two hundred yards away now, was facing him, its barrel inviting. He wondered if he was pushing his luck a little.

He took the pencil grenade out of the breach of the Carlson, removed its delayed-action fuse so that it would explode on impact, and took careful aim.

He fired. He dropped down at once, and covered his head. He heard the gun go up as the grenade went down its barrel, spewing its metal intestines out in a burst of brilliant red flame. He felt the blast of it roll him over and over, and he saw splintered steel twisting through the air, a giant column of smoke that was thick with splintering shards. A severed leg was hurtling towards him, and he stared at it in fascination, watching it fall close beside him; the temptation to pick it up and wave it like a banner was almost insuperable.

And as he gaped, he saw young woman, a swarthy, black-eyed woman, racing towards him, firing her machine pistol as she ran. The bullets cut across his legs, and he fell. As he rolled over he fired his second grenade and watched it go through her breast and out at the back, embedding itself into a tree. Twelve seconds later it exploded and blew her dead body to shreds.

He said sourly, gasping, "Tough luck, baby..."

Both his legs were broken, and he was losing blood fast. He took out his Med-Kit, put a tourniquet on each thigh, and began to drag himself slowly, in acute pain, back to his position.

It was Gopa who came to bring him in, running fast and low, hoisting the giant burden onto his narrow shoulders and running back with it, dropping him down once more into the foxhole and saying, "The trouble with you bastards is, you don't have any sense. You weren't supposed to get hurt..."

He felt the Irish whiskey trickling down his throat, and he clutched at his groin and said weakly, "The balls, make sure she didn't get my balls..."

He heard Gopa say, tearing at the uniform those, "Don't worry—if she did, you can have one of mine—I don't need them both..." And then he passed into unconsciousness.

Gopa picked up the sender and said, "He's back, Major," and Bramble said, "Mortars, resume firing."

The battle went on, and for thirty minutes the air reverberated with the fury of it. When at last the mortars ceased their pounding, the Kalashnikovs were silent too.

Paul said, "Now. This is when the survivors will come at us."

They waited. In a few moments half a hundred men, in a long and ragged line, were forcing their suicidal way, waist deep, through the swamp. They were firing their machine pistols as they came, a prolonged and steady fusillade that cut through the trees and thudded into the earthworks with the sickening sound of finality.

Bramble was watching, He had taken a bullet in the left arm, and the blood was dripping from his wrist, trickling down the leg of his pants. "Units Five and Seven only, move forward to the right flank, open fire when you're ready. All other Units remain under cover," he ordered.

It was slaughter now—the final accounting. The barrage went on, uselessly, as Five and Seven ran forward to their new position, outflanking the attackers. They dropped down into the mud and opened fire, and the enemy line began to move around to face them.

Bramble said, "All Units. Carlsons only, open fire."

The glasses were at his eyes, and he was watching the battle, seeing the line thin out as the Carlsons cut them to pieces. He swung the glasses round, watched for a moment, and said calmly, "Kirby."

Simon Kirby, the blood gushing from a deep wound in his neck—was it a mortar fragment that was jaggedly sticking out of him there?—was running fast towards them, his gun chattering, a solitary man with a desperate rage in him, mouthing soundless phrases as he moved.

Paul Tobin switched his rifle to single and raised it to his shoulder.

He saw Kirby fall and swung round to face the rear, the sound of the single-shot Kalashnikov a sudden shock. Beside him, Bramble had swung around too, and was staring. He said quietly; "That Indian's a pretty fancy shot, right through the black patch where his left eye used to be..."

Flagstaff was stalking out from the cover of the trees, coming slowly towards them; his stolen gun loosely held now. He stood there for a moment, fifty yards away, the mist shrouding him, a ghost. His head was cocked back a little, and he was looking at them with a taut and angry look on his face. They saw him turn his eyes from one side to the other, as all down the line, the men of the Private Army began to rise up from their foxholes, like the shades of dead men rising from the earth.

The Indian took a long, deep breath, and said nothing. Then he turned and went silently back to the shelter of the trees.

Arthur Reddies was shouting, "Captain? Captain Strickland?"

He hacked at the creepers all around him with his unaccustomed machete, biting a way through the green, living mass of it. He heard someone shout, "Hey, Art, is that you?" and he called back angrily, "Yes, it's me, where's the Chief?"

"Isn't he with you?"

"Oh, for Christ sake..."

He could hear the men laboring their way along, see some of them from time to time when the vegetation opened up and the mist lay lower over the swamp. He waited till one of them came over to him, and asked again, "Chet, where's Strickland?"

The man shook his head, breathing heavily, trying to get his wind again. He said, "My Christ, are we still in the State of Florida?" He stumbled on, swinging his blade, enlarging the path the Indians had cut. Reddies moved over to the side and shouted out again, "Captain? Chief? Where are you?"

But Captain Strickland did not answer. He was lying under a low canopy of moss, more than a mile further back, hidden from the rest of the world and groaning. Close beside him, Colonel Tobin was standing patiently, waiting for him to recover, standing there with his feet wide-spread, his arms folded, his chin sunk on his chest.

And when at last Strickland opened his eyes and looked around for his rifle, the Colonel unsung it from his shoulder and said pleasantly, "I have it, Captain. You won't need it now." As Strickland made a fast movement towards his holster, he added. "Your revolver too..."

The pain in his head was excruciating, but he pulled himself to his feet and looked at his own revolver, held lightly in the Colonel's hand and not threatening him, and decided not to charge and pummel him down into the swamp. He stood his ground, and said, "What happened?"

He was getting ready, testing himself, waiting his opportunity, and the Colonel said easily, "What happened? I'm afraid I hit you. I had to separate you from your men, so I sneaked up and hit you on the back of the neck. Not very hard—it'll soon wear off."

Strickland stared at him. He put a hand to the back of his head, grimaced, and thought, *I'll teach the sonofabitch, I'll break him in two.*

"Are you thinking of trying to disarm me?" asked Colonel Tobin. "I do believe you are."

Quite unexpectedly, he tossed the revolver over. Strickland caught it and flipped open the chamber to make sure that it was still fully loaded. It was. He shot out both his hands, the gun held tight and pointed straight at the Colonel's face; there was a violent anger in his eyes.

The Colonel grimaced. "I told you, you don't need a gun. I'm not one of Kirby's mob, you know. It should be obvious to you."

"It should? Just tell me why?"

"I'm not the type."

"Uh-huh. So tell me who you are."

The Colonel shrugged. "I'm Colonel Tobin. I don't imagine you've ever heard of me...Or have you? Yes, I see you have. Well, we've just finished the job that we came here to do, the job you once started."

He could not hide his astonishment. The two men stood in the damp gray mist, facing each other and not moving. Strickland said, "Well, I'll be a sonofabitch...Now put your hands up, nice and slow, you're coming with me."

"No, I'm not, as a matter of fact. I have a few things to tell you, and then I'll be on my way and leave you in peace."

Strickland was shaking with fury. He cocked the hammer on the revolver and said, "Put your goddam hands in the air!"

For a little while, the Colonel watched him, seeing the anger there and knowing that it could be dangerous. He shook his head, very slowly, and said quietly, "Just listen to me, Strickland. Just hear me out."

The moment of danger was gone. Strickland lowered the gun, held it in one hand now, pointed at the Colonel's belly. He took a deep breath and said curtly, "I'll listen."

"Good. Do you know a place called Wishalokee Creek? Nine and one-half miles due south of here?"

"I know it."

"You'll find Simon Kirby there. It seems that someone put a bullet right through his eyepatch; it blew the back of his head off. A Kalashnikov bullet—you know the damage they do. Dum-dum. You'll find a lot of other bodies there too, our own body count was a hundred and ninety-four, but there may be others. The rest of them will all have dispersed by now, and I don't really think you'll have any more trouble from them. The CAAA does not really exist anymore. Any questions?"

Strickland was trying to puzzle it all out, hating every minute of it. He said slowly, "I got a report from the SS. Seems like somebody tipped them off about a guy by the name of Buzz Friendly. Seems he's been stalking the Chief Executive for a while. You know anything about that?"

"Yes. One of my people made that phone call."

"Uh-huh."

"That Pan Am hijacking that never came off?"

"My people too. And all the rest as well. We picked up a girl named Carolyne Southby. I believe you know about her."

"The Southby woman? Yes, I know her. Where is she?"

"I have got her hidden away. I'm smuggling her out of the country."

"You're handing her over to me, Tobin."

"*Colonel* Tobin, if you don't mind, Captain. No, I'm sending her into a sort of...exile, I suppose you'd call it?" He smiled, very affably, the pale blue eyes still hard as steel. "So you won't have to worry about her anymore, either."

Captain Strickland gestured with the revolver and said angrily, "You don't really believe I've got a gun in my hand, do you?"

"Shall we say, I don't really believe you've any intention

of using it? Why should you?" There was a touch of mockery in his voice, and he said, "You've just covered yourself with glory, Captain Strickland, isn't that nice?"

"How's that?" He hated the clipped, concise British accent, hated the sardonic arrogance.

The Colonel was motionless as a tree stump, rooted there. "I've had a word on your behalf with Arthur Wagnall in Washington. I told him your foray into the swamp, in direct disobedience to his orders, was at my own instigation, so you'd better make that your story too. I don't really like lying in my teeth like that, but under the circumstances...Yes, I think I would have done the same thing. Oh, he'll grumble a lot about the chain of command, all that sort of nonsense, but when you hand him Simon Kirby's head on a silver platter, he'll wonder how you managed to get it and say no more about it."

He added drily, "You'll be a hero, Strickland."

For a long, long time, nobody spoke. The fog was closing around them, surging. At last, the Captain put his gun away. He said tightly, "I'll take my rifle too, if you don't mind."

The Colonel handed it to him, and said gently, "I'm deeply sorry about your lady, Strickland. I'm sorry that we couldn't have prevented it. Please give her my deepest sympathies."

There was another moment of silence, and Strickland nodded. "I'll do that, Colonel."

"Is she going to be all right?"

"Yes."

"I'm glad. Good-day, Captain."

Without another word, he turned and walked off, a slight and agile figure with a look about him that could only be described as jaunty.

Strickland watched him go until the trees and the floating, nebulous spindrift of the mist had closed about him. He said again, aloud, "Well, I'll be a sonofabitch..."

* * *

The darkness was impenetrable, a clammy, clouded sky with the threat of rain in it, as black as the mud at their feet as the hundred men of Colonel Tobin's Private Army made their way down to the beach.

Out there, beyond the mouth of the Shark River, the *Maya* was riding at anchor. Close inshore, among the low-lying islets and the gently swaying chumps of kelp, the black rubber boats had been drawn up onto the dark sand.

They were watching the men embark, silently, and Colonel Tobin said, "I don't want you to stay too long, Paul."

Paul Tobin nodded. "Just long enough to do what I have to do. I want to make sure they're going to be all right. The doctor says a few more days, a week perhaps..."

"And then?"

"Flagstaff will take care of them. That's all he's ever wanted to do. They'll go back to the houseboat, the three of them...It's not much of a life, but they're satisfied with it, and that's all that matters."

Rick Meyers said, "He'll take good care of them, Colonel."

He was staring out into the darkness of the sea, watching the gray surf breaking, his moody, somber eyes grave and thoughtful, remembering.

The Colonel said abruptly, "All right, let's get on with it. That's our dinghy."

He helped Pamela Charles and Betty de Haas aboard, then took his son's hand and shook it, saying, "I'll give you ten days, Paul. No more."

"Ten days is enough, Dad. Have a good trip home."

He watched the line of the boats rocking gently over the surf and turned away with a sigh. Slowly, deep in thought, he walked up the beach and into the timeless swamp.

THE END

ABOUT THE AUTHOR

Alan Lyle-Smythe was born in Surrey, England. Prior to World War II, he served with the Palestine Police from 1936 to 1939 and learned the Arabic language. He was awarded an MBE in June 1938. He married Aliza Sverdova in 1939, then studied acting from 1939 to 1941.

In January 1940, Lyle-Smythe was commissioned in the Royal Army Service Corps. Due to his linguistic skills, he transferred to the Intelligence Corps and served in the Western Desert, in which he used the surname "Caillou" (the French word for 'pebble') as an alias.

He was captured in North Africa, imprisoned and threatened with execution in Italy, then escaped to join the British forces at Salerno. He was then posted to serve with the partisans in Yugoslavia. He wrote about his experiences in the book *The World is Six Feet Square* (1954). He was promoted to captain and awarded the Military Cross in 1944.

Following the war, he returned to the Palestine Police from 1946 to 1947, then served as a Police Commissioner in British-occupied Italian Somaliland from 1947 to 1952, where he was recommissioned a captain.

After work as a District Officer in Somalia and professional hunter, Lyle-Smythe travelled to Canada, where he worked as a hunter and then became an actor on Canadian television.

He wrote his first novel, *Rogue's Gambit*, in 1955, first using the name Caillou, one of his aliases from the war. Moving from Vancouver to Hollywood, he made an appearance as a contestant on the January 23 1958 edition of *You Bet Your Life*.

He appeared as an actor and/or worked as a screenwriter in such shows as *Daktari*, *The Man From U.N.C.L.E.* (including the screenwriting for "*The Bow-Wow Affair*" from 1965), *Thriller*, *Daniel Boone*, *Quark*, *Centennial*, and *How the West Was Won*. In 1966-67, he had a recurring role (as Jason Flood) in NBC's "*Tarzan*" TV series starring Ron Ely. Caillou appeared in such television movies as *Sole Survivor* (1970), *The Hound of the Baskervilles* (1972, as Inspector Lestrade), and *Goliath Awaits* (1981). His cinema film credits included roles in *Five Weeks in a Balloon* (1962), *Clarence, the Cross-Eyed Lion* (1965), *The Rare Breed* (1966), *The Devil's Brigade* (1968), *Hellfighters* (1968), *Everything You Always Wanted to Know About Sex* (*But Were Afraid to Ask)* (1972), *Herbie Goes to Monte Carlo* (1977), *Beyond Evil* (1980), *The Sword and the Sorcerer* (1982) and *The Ice Pirates* (1984).

Caillou wrote 52 paperback thrillers under his own name and the nom de plume of Alex Webb, with such heroes as Cabot Cain, Colonel Matthew Tobin, Mike Benasque, Ian Quayle and Josh Dekker, as well as writing many magazine stories.

Several of Caillou's novels were made into films, such as *Rampage* with Robert Mitchum in 1963, based on his big game hunting knowledge; *Assault on Agathon*, for which Caillou did the screenplay as well; and *The Cheetahs*, filmed in 1989.

He was married to Aliza Sverdova from 1939 until his death. Their daughter Nadia Caillou was the screenwriter for the film *Skeleton Coast*.

Alan Caillou died in Sedona, Arizona in 2006.

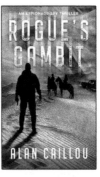
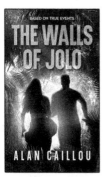

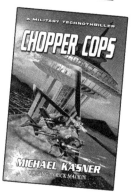

DON'T MISS ANY OF NEIL HUNTER'S NOVELS FROM CALIBER BOOKS

Reporter Les Mason is completing an expose on the Long Point Nuclear Plant. But before he can finish he dies an agonizing death. The doctors are baffled—and there are similar cases to follow...Chris Lane, his girlfriend, and organizer of the Long Point Protestors, discovers Mason's notes, and decides to find out for herself what the plant has to hide.

2 BOOK SERIES

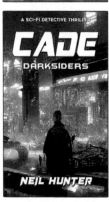

In middle of the 21st century America – over-populated decaying cities are ruled by hi-tech gangs pushing every vice and wastelands are controlled by bands of mutants. Ordinary citizens are oppressed and face a hopeless future. But Marshal T.J. Cade is a new breed of law enforcer. Teamed with his cyborg partner, Janek, Cade takes on these criminals and works in the gray areas of the law to get the job done.

3 BOOK SERIES

The village of Shepthorne England wasn't being gripped, but strangled by a winter's blanket of heavy snow and Arctic temperatures. The trouble began innocently enough with a massive pile-up of autos on frozen roads leading to and from the village. Then, from the sky, a military transport plane with its top secret cargo of devastation crashed down towards the center of the village. Hell was just beginning to touch Shepthorne and its unsuspecting citizens...

FROM CALIBER BOOKS

CALIBER BOOKS

CALIBER COMICS GOES TO WAR!
HISTORICAL AND MILITARY THEMED GRAPHIC NOVELS

**WORLD WAR ONE:
MO MAN'S LAND**

ISBN: 9781635298123

*A look at World War 1 from
the French trenches as they
faced the Imperial German
Army.*

**CORTEZ AND THE FALL
OF THE AZTECS**

ISBN: 9781635299779

*Cortez battles the Aztecs
while in search of Inca
gold.*

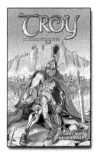

**TROY:
AN EMPIRE UNDER SIEGE**

ISBN: 9781635298635

*Homer's famous The Iliad and
the Trojan War is given a
unique human perspective
rather than from the God's.*

WITNESS TO WAR

ISBN: 9781635299700

*WW2's Battle of the Bulge
is seen up close by an
embedded female war
reporter.*

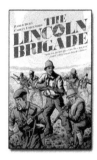

THE LINCOLN BRIGADE

ISBN: 9781635298222

*American volunteers head
to Spain in the 1930s to
fight in their civil war
against the fascist regime.*

**EL CID:
THE CONQUEROR**

ISBN: 9780982654996

*Europe's greatest warrior
attempts to unify Spain
against invading foreign
and domestic armies.*

WINTER WAR

ISBN: 9780985749392

*At the outbreak of WW2
Finland fights against an
invading Soviet army.*

**ZULUNATION:
END OF EMPIRE**

ISBN: 9780941613415

*The global British Empire
and far-reaching influence
is threatened by a Zulu
uprising in southern Africa.*

AIR WARRIORS: WORLD WAR ONE #V1 - V4   *Take to the skys of WW1 as various fighter aces tell their harrowing stories.*
ISBN: 9781635297973 (V1), 9781635297980 (V2), 9781635297997 (V3), 9781635298000 (V4)

CALIBER COMICS GOES TO THE EDGE!
Science Fiction and Horror themed graphic novels

DEADWORLD
ISBN: 9781942351245

RENFIELD
ISBN: 9781942351825

NOSFERATU
ISBN: 9781942351931

**LOVECRAFT:
THE EARLY STORIES**
ISBN: 9781942351634

**THE WAR OF THE WORLDS:
INFESTATION**
ISBN: 9781942351962

TIME GRUNTS
ISBN: 9781635299472

DRACULA
ISBN: 9780996030649

**DRACULA:
THE SUICIDE CLUB**
ISBN: 9781635299571

**JACK THE RIPPER
ILLUSTRATED**
ISBN: 9781942351917

THE SEARCHERS
ISBN: 9781942351979

A.A.I. WARS
ISBN: 9781635299168

**AUTUMN: TERROR IN THE
LONDON UNDERGROUND**
ISBN: 9781544624020

www.calibercomics.com

THE STORY OF SCOTT 'JOURNAL' NEITHAMMER DOESN'T END WITH VIETNAM JOURNAL

'JOURNAL' HEADS TO THE PERSIAN GULF TO COVER THE FIRST GULF WAR CONFLICT

August 1, 1990, Saddam Hussein, with his eye on the rich oil fields of Kuwait rolled his army into that neighboring country with the intention of annexing Kuwait as a province, while claiming its riches for himself. War was brewing once again on the American horizon. Scott 'Journal' Neithammer comes out of retirement to cover the first Persian Gulf War. He finds himself also caught up in the war between the Pentagon and the press! Fed up with press restrictions, he heads off into the desert on his own - and gets an unwelcome first hand taste of the full fury of modern American firepower!

"First rate...alternates documentary-style reporting with documentary-style fiction. One of the five best war comics."
- *Don Thompson, The Comics Buyer's Guide.*

"Stresses authenticity. Anyone who saw the real city of Khafji in Saudi Arabia will recognize landmarks in the comic book."
- *Ron Jensen, The Stars and Stripes.*

NOW AVAILABLE

GULF WAR JOURNAL: BOOK ONE DESERT STORM

GULF WAR JOURNAL: BOOK TWO GROUND WAR

WRITTEN AND ILLUSTRATED BY DON LOMAX

www.calibercomics.com

ALSO AVAILABLE FROM DON LOMAX

HIGH SHINING BRASS

High Shining Brass is based on the true story of an American spy during the Vietnam War as told to Don Lomax by agent Robert Durand who chronicles the tale. Durand was a member of a black-ops team, code- named "Shining Brass." The series depicts the horrific atrocities witnessed and performed by the once naïve special forces member as he attempts to perform his duties and understand the true meaning behind the madness. Durand's group was under the command of a combined force, comprised of every branch of the services, and headed up by the ever-popular Central Intelligence Committee. It's a journey into a shadow world of treachery and deceit—and reveals the way lives of Americans were traded about carelessly during the war in Vietnam.

ISBN: 978-1544962191 $14.99US

ABOVE AND BEYOND

Beginning in May of 2007, noted comic writer and illustrator Don Lomax teamed up with Police and Security News magazine to produce the series "Above and Beyond" - real life depictions of heroic acts by law enforcement professionals. Just as our soldiers here and abroad deserve recognition for their unwavering service, so do the men and women who protect and serve the citizens of the United States. Contained within these pages are just a few stories of these individuals who have demonstrated selfless bravery and heroic action under the most difficult circumstances and gone above and beyond the call of duty.

ISBN: 978-1635299601 $ 9.99 US

ALSO AVAILABLE FROM CALIBER COMICS

QUALITY GRAPHIC NOVELS TO ENTERTAIN

THE SEARCHERS: VOLUME 1
The Shape of Things to Come

Before *League of Extraordinary Gentlemen* there was *The Searchers*. At the dawn of the 20th Century the greatest literary adventurers from the minds of Wells, Doyle, Burroughs, and Haggard were created. All thought to be the work of pure fiction. However, a century later, the real-life descendents of those famous characters are reunited by the legendary Professor Challenger in order to save mankind's future. Series collected for the first time.

"Searchers is the comic book I have on the wall with a sign reading · 'Love books? Never read a comic? Try this one! ....money back guarantee..." · Dark Star Books.

WAR OF THE WORLDS: INFESTATION

Based on the H.G. Wells classic! The "Martian Invasion" has begun again and now mankind must fight for its very humanity. It happened slowly at first but by the third year, it seemed that the war was almost over... the war was almost lost.

"Writer Randy Zimmerman has a fine grasp of drama, and spins the various strands of the story into a coherent whole... imaginative and very gritty." - war-of-the-worlds.co.uk

HELSING: LEGACY BORN

From writer Gary Reed (Deadworld) and artists John Lowe (Captain America), Bruce McCorkindale (Godzilla). She was born into a legacy she wanted no part of and pushed into a battle recessed deep in the shadows of the night. Samantha Helsing is torn between two worlds...two allegiances...two families. The legacy of the Van Helsing family and their crusade against the "night creatures" comes to modern day with the most unlikely of all warriors.

"Congratulations on this masterpiece..." - Paul Dale Roberts, Compuserve Reviews

DEADWORLD

Before there was The Walking Dead there was Deadworld. Here is an introduction of the long running classic horror series, Deadworld, to a new audience! Considered by many to be the godfather of the original zombie comic with over 100 issues and graphic novels in print and over 1,000,000 copies sold, Deadworld ripped into the undead with intelligent zombies on a mission and a group of poor teens riding in a school bus desperately try to stay one step ahead of the sadistic, Harley-riding King Zombie. Death, mayhem, and a touch of supernatural evil made Deadworld a classic and now here's your chance to get into the story!

DAYS OF WRATH

Award winning comic writer & artist Wayne Vansant brings his gripping World War II saga of war in the Pacific to Guadalcanal and the Battle of Bloody Ridge. This is the powerful story of the long, vicious battle for Guadalcanal that occurred in 1942-43. When the U.S. Navy orders its outnumbered and out-gunned ships to run from the Japanese fleet, they abandon American troops on a bloody, battered island in the South Pacific.

"Heavy on authenticity, compellingly written and beautifully drawn." - Comics Buyers Guide

SHERLOCK HOLMES:
THE CASE OF THE MISSING MARTIAN

Sherlock is called out of retirement to London in 1908 to solve a most baffling mystery: The British Museum is missing a specimen of a Martian from the failed invasion of 1899. Did it walk away on its own or did someone steal it?

Holmes ponders the facts and remembers his part in the war effort alongside Professor Challenger during the War of the Worlds invasion that was chronicled in H.G. Wells' classic novel.

Meanwhile, Doctor Watson has problems of his own when his wife steals a scalpel from his surgical tool kit and returns to her old stomping grounds of Whitechapel, the London

CALIBER PRESENTS

The original Caliber Presents anthology title was one of Caliber's inaugural releases and featured predominantly new creators, many of which went onto successful careers in the comics' industry. In this new version, Caliber Presents has expanded to graphic novel size and while still featuring new creators it also includes many established professional creators with new visions. Creators featured in this first issue include nominees and winners of some of the industry's major awards including the Eisner, Harvey, Xeric, Ghastly, Shel Dorf, Comic Monsters, and more.

LEGENDLORE

From Caliber Comics now comes the entire Realm and Legendlore saga as a set of volumes that collects the long running critically acclaimed series. In the vein of The Lord of The Rings and The Hobbit with elements of Game of Thrones and Dungeon and Dragons.

Four normal modern day teenagers are plunged into a world they thought only existed in novels and film. They are whisked away to a magical land where dragons roam the skies, orcs and hobgoblins terrorize travelers, where unicorns prance through the forest, and kingdoms wage war for dominance. It is a world where man is just one race, joining other races such as elves, trolls, dwarves, changelings, and the dreaded night creatures who steal the night.

TIME GRUNTS

What if Hitler's last great Super Weapon was – Time itself! A WWII/time travel adventure that can best be described as Band of Brothers meets Time Bandits.

October, 1944. Nazi fortunes appear bleaker by the day. But in the bowels of the Wenceslas Mines, a terrible threat has emerged . . . The Nazis have discovered the ability to conquer time itself with the help of a new ominous device!

Now a rag tag group of American GIs must stop this threat to the past, present, and future . . . While dealing with their own past, prejudices, and fears in the process.

CALIBER
C O M I C S

www.calibercomics.com

Milton Keynes UK
Ingram Content Group UK Ltd.
UKHW020914220424
441551UK00017B/1149